The telegram from Katie McKay just said MUST TALK. STOP.

But when Seth Cooper read it, sitting by a fire in a jungle on the other side of the world, he knew she was *really* saying...

BABY COMING. STOP. REMEMBER WHAT YOU PROMISED ME. STOP. THIS BABY DESERVES A FATHER NOT JUST A MOTHER. STOP.

And then there was what it meant to *him*....

STOP YOUR CAREFREE INDEPENDENT BACHELOR LIFE. STOP TRAVELING THE WORLD AND COME HOME AND BE A MAKE-BELIEVE HUSBAND FOR KATIE McKAY AND A REAL FATHER FOR HER BABY. STOP THINKING ABOUT HOW YOU'VE ALWAYS WANTED HER SO BADLY YOU COULD TASTE IT. AND WHEN YOU START THINKING ABOUT WANTING TO BE A REAL HUSBAND TO THIS BEAUTIFUL DESIRABLE CHARMING WOMAN FOR GOD'S SAKE JUST STOP.

Dear Reader,

I remember when I first discovered Greek food. I was in college, and there was a Greek restaurant one door down the street from my apartment. The moment my boyfriend took me there and bought me my first souvlaki, I was in love. Not with him, mind you. (That—foolishly!—came later.) With souvlaki. And moussaka. And pastitsio. Not to mention baklava. I continue to love Greek food to this day, so it's no mystery to me why Jared Panetta, who first encounters Demi Tripopulous when he wants to buy the family restaurant, should not only fall in love with Demi's Greek delicacies but with the woman herself. Soon enough, he's making her *The Offer She Couldn't Refuse.* And for your sake, I hope you don't refuse this newest delight from award-winning author Marie Ferrarella.

Of course, you also shouldn't miss Christie Ridgway's latest: *Ready, Set...Baby!* There's just something about a marriage-of-convenience plot that I can't resist. And luckily for readers everywhere, heroine Katie McKay is equally unable to resist hero Seth Cooper. And it's not just the baby on the way making her feel romantic—it's the man himself. He's a winner—and so is this book.

I hope you enjoy both these wonderful novels, and I also hope you'll come back next month for two more wonderful Yours Truly books all about unexpectedly meeting, dating—and marrying!—Mr. Right.

Yours,

Leslie J. Wainger
Senior Editor and Editorial Coordinator

Please address questions and book requests to:
Silhouette Reader Service
U.S.: 3010 Walden Ave., P.O. Box 1325, Buffalo, NY 14269
Canadian: P.O. Box 609, Fort Erie, Ont. L2A 5X3

CHRISTIE RIDGWAY

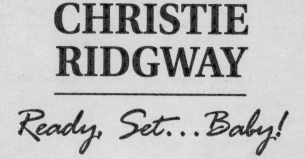

Ready, Set...Baby!

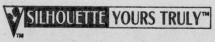

SILHOUETTE YOURS TRULY™

Published by Silhouette Books

America's Publisher of Contemporary Romance

For Sally Tyler Hayes. Thanks for holding my
hand and lighting the way.

 SILHOUETTE BOOKS

ISBN 0-373-52062-X

READY, SET...BABY!

About the author

CHRISTIE RIDGWAY fell in love with romance novels as a girl, when she spent all her allowance money on romances and red licorice vines. Now, in Southern California, she fulfills her dream of being a published author. Work time is only occasionally (ha!) interrupted by her two young sons. In addition to writing, she volunteers at her children's school and loves to read and cook.

Christie credits her happiness to the smarts she used in picking her husband, Rob.

Christie loves to hear from her readers. Contact her at P.O. Box 3803, La Mesa, CA 91944.

Books by Christie Ridgway

Silhouette Yours Truly

The Wedding Date
Follow That Groom!
Have Baby, Will Marry
Ready, Set...Baby!

1

Was she pregnant or wasn't she?

The $64,000 question—better make that $64 million—hung over Seth Cooper's head like the glistening blade of a guillotine.

He gripped the wheel of the rented Ford Explorer and stared across the street at Katie McKay's large, farm-style house. Paisley drapes swooped casually across the front window of the San Francisco Peninsula home. A Bunyan-size fir tree dominated the front yard; a carefully weeded patch of pansies surrounded a brass mailbox on a wooden post. Not one of these gave the slightest hint as to whether or not the occupant was pregnant.

Heck, Cooper, what did you expect?

"I don't know," he murmured back to himself. "A big banner proclaiming The Rabbit Lives?"

His inner voice actually snorted. *That's not how they figure it out these days, fool. They use those little sticks that you—you—*

"That you what?" Seth squeezed the steering wheel. That was how out of touch with pregnancy and babies he was. Even his subconscious didn't know what you did with those little sticks. Not like a thermometer, were they?

He squeezed the steering wheel again, then forced his fingers to relax. None of this would answer the question. It was just that he'd never expected to face this problem. When his brother Ryan had shared the facts of his wife Karen's infertility, Seth had been embarrassed, then somewhat awed by the lengths they were willing to go to have a child.

But the car crash that had ended Ryan's and Karen's lives two months ago—Seth blocked the familiar crush of sadness—had also ended their dream of a family.

And possibly had left Karen's sister, Katie McKay, pregnant with Ryan and Karen's child.

What were the odds that one shot at in vitro fertilization had impregnated her?

Sighing, he reached into his pocket, fingers touching the telegram Katie had sent that had found him in a smoky hut in Vietnam. Yet what were the odds that Katie McKay's cryptic "Must Talk," meant anything but?

No more procrastinating. He'd received the telegram two days ago, but he'd hidden from this and every other problem resulting from his brother's death for the past two months. In five weeks he had to face a tableful of board of directors and show them that his and Ryan's company rested in capable hands.

Unfolding from behind the wheel, Seth forced himself out of the car, across the street and up the walkway. The time had come to deal with all the problems—speedily, efficiently. Then he could make his way back to Asia, Europe, Africa—wherever his feet wandered.

On Katie's doorstep he paused, an unexpected lick of anticipation traveling his spine. Five years ago, he'd met Katie McKay and felt...something. They'd danced, the "something" had turned sizzling, then was extinguished as soon as the bridal bouquet was tossed. That little ritual had quickly brought him to his senses.

The memory dissolved as he fingered the telegram again. With his other hand he rang the bell and listened. Light, nonpregnant-specific footsteps. The door opened. And there stood Katie.

As if he'd hit air turbulence, his gut did a jerky slide-and-bump. Sexual awareness sidled up to his libido and elbowed it to life. Roaring life. *Oh, I don't need this.*

Somehow, the memory of Katie's striking looks had grown hazy in his mind over the past five years. She was fair, about five-seven and slender. Her ice-blond hair was blunt-cut to chin length, framing perfect cheekbones and a perfectly straight, small nose. She had the clean, timeless look of forever and always.

Seth forced his gaze away from the arresting beauty of her face to take in her white sneakers, jeans, and long-tailed denim shirt that nearly brushed her knees.

Then, against his will, his eyes moved back to her face.

Crack. Another flash of man-woman awareness jolted him.

Instantly followed by a sluicing rush of relief.

Cross one problem off the list.

A dozen things might have prompted Katie's telegram, but pregnancy couldn't be one of them. A pregnant near-stranger couldn't possibly turn him on.

He smiled. His libido—and well-honed sense of self-preservation—were too smart for that.

Katie McKay stared at the man on her doorstep, her hand tightly clutching the brass doorknob.

He—Seth Cooper—suddenly smiled and his tense pose relaxed. *Her* stomach quivered like gelatin. "Seth," she said. "I'd forgotten how much you're like Ryan."

With that stellar remark out, she hastily opened the door wider and gestured him in. Still faintly smiling, he stepped up and over the threshold and then Katie remembered Seth wasn't that much like Ryan after all. Although there was the same set to the emerald-green eyes, although both men had the same honey-brown hair, Ryan hadn't been nearly Seth's size. Rugged and broad-shouldered, Seth was a shaggy mountain of a man.

She ignored another nervous quiver of her stomach. She'd spotted other differences in Ryan the moment she'd met Seth that long-ago wedding day. Seth had a dangerous restlessness. A one-eye-on-the-door attitude that had warned her away from him. Warned her to ignore the enticing burn when his fingers entwined with hers, and to ignore the sensation of his hot, hard palm on her back as they danced.

To be on the safe side, she'd made sure she never met him again. Until now.

"I have coffee in the kitchen. Follow me." She'd been drinking her usual herbal tea, of course, but she had the remains of the pot she'd made for her business partner, Izzy. Her news might be better shared across the benign expanse of the kitchen table.

She stole a quick look at him and shook her head slightly. *How can he be so calm, so cool?*

Their brief-but-indelible past encounter, the problematic present and the utter who-could-have-known quality of the future generated an atmosphere that for her, at least, was thick with tension. She could barely wade through it as she led the way from the living room to the large kitchen at the back.

A small fire burned in the room's waist-high brick fireplace—practically the whole reason she'd chosen this house. That and the fact that it had a detached office she'd converted to a separate kitchen for Katie's Candies, her gourmet-chocolates business.

He took one of the seats in the breakfast nook, the round table in front of him littered with files, cookbooks, and her laptop computer. "Excuse the mess," she said, her voice dry from nervousness. "I run my business from my home, so there's stuff every-where.''

"No problem," Seth said, leaning back in the chair, obviously relaxed. "What is it you do, again? Something with food?"

She smiled, glad to avoid the all-important subject a few seconds longer. "I hand-make specialty choc-olates." She crossed to the counter and poured coffee into a cup for him.

"You don't look like Betty Crocker."

Katie didn't know how to take the remark. *He* looked like an adventurer; all romantic possibilities and hard-muscled hunkiness.

Which was exactly what he was, she supposed, as a buyer for Ends of the Earth, the catalog company he'd owned with his brother. Seth wandered the world, searching out the unusual and unique—items as diverse as handcrafted wood-carver's knives from Africa to handwoven, hand-sewn backpacks from Ti-bet—all wildly popular.

But she had to tell him why she'd telegrammed. That certainty made her set his coffee mug in front of him with a telltale anxious clatter.

Katie sighed. *Oh, Karen, wherever you are, help me out.* The thought of her sister calmed her ner-vousness. Karen and Ryan's senseless death had pro-duced dark feelings that Katie had found seductively easy to wallow in, until the doctor's verdict a month ago. The news he'd given her had brought purpose, hope, *life* back to her world.

She filled her teacup from the fragrant pot on the counter and pulled out the chair beside him, settling into it, then scraping it up to the table. *I have to tell him.*

From beneath her lashes she darted him a quick look. He stared into his coffee cup, then lifted his head and gazed at the wall. Frames covered it, frames filled with pictures of the family. She watched his eyes roam from one to another. Karen, Ryan. Karen, Ryan and Katie last Christmas. Individual shots of her parents, separated, of course, by a good six feet of plaster. Amazing they could even share the same wall.

"Katie, I—"

"Seth, I—"

They both stopped, then laughed—his low, hers nervous. A little silence descended over the table. She took a fortifying sip of tea. "So, Seth, how are you? About Karen and Ryan, I mean." She couldn't just blurt out the truth, not with him looking so relaxed. "You doing okay?"

He grimaced. "I'm all right."

The hint of concealed pain in his voice crumpled her heart like a piece of paper in his big fist. Katie involuntarily bit her lip, needing a pain to mask the sting in her eyes. "I know," she whispered.

The grimace evened out. "And I'm getting better." He paused, staring into his mug. "I've been all over the world, Katie, and I've seen a lot of things I don't understand. But I go on. I'm still walking and eating. I still wonder who's going to win the Super Bowl."

He looked at her with a half grin. "Wile E. Coyote and the Road Runner still make me smile."

Warmth flowered in Katie's chest. "Bugs," she corrected gently. "I've always liked Bugs Bunny best."

It was going to be all right. Seth was a reasonable, normal human being.

She would just explain the situation to him. Tell him that she carried Ryan and Karen's baby, but since Ryan and Karen weren't there to be its parents, well... Well, she would explain her plan about that after he'd gotten used to the idea of the pregnancy.

"Seth—"

Her front door slammed open. "Ho! Who's home?" a boisterous voice boomed.

Katie's stomach dropped to her toes. "Dan! Back here in the kitchen." Dan Hughes, the husband of her partner Izzy, knew she was pregnant. What if he spilled the beans before she could—

"Miss K.!" Like a big, friendly Labrador retriever, Dan galloped into the room and bussed her on the cheek. "How are you—"

She interrupted before he gave anything away. "Fine, fine. Izzy's gone out on an errand."

Dan grinned. "Don't try to fool me. Another fast-food french-fry craving?" He looked down at her stomach. "What about you? Do you—"

"Have you met Seth Cooper?" She interrupted him again hastily, gesturing toward the corner chair.

Dan halted, obviously becoming aware of the other

man for the first time. Surprise turned to a delighted grin on his face. "Seth, you crazy SOB!"

Seth had risen from his chair, and with a quieter version of Dan's smile on his face, he shook hands. "Right back at you, Dan. How've you been?"

"Great, just great." Dan sobered. "But not so great for you, huh? I'm sorry about Ryan and Karen."

Seth shoved his hands into his pockets. "Thanks. I'm doing okay, though."

"Well, I should say so!" Good humor revving up again, Dan glanced between Seth and Katie. "I mean, what with—"

"Dan!" Katie grabbed his arm tightly. "I need you to do me a little favor. Outside."

"What?" Dan looked bewildered. As dear as he was, subtleties went right over his head.

"Outside." Katie squeezed his forearm.

"Okay, okay." Izzy must have been working on him, because he let her lead him off. "Hey, give me a call," he yelled over his shoulder to Seth. Dan grinned again, looking down at Katie. "I'm jazzed to see him. He's been my best friend since we were little kids."

It took just a couple of minutes to cram Dan back into his car. When she returned to the kitchen, she found Seth still seated at the table.

He looked up as she entered the room and met her gaze. A current of awareness passed between them, and like it was just this minute and not five years ago, she felt again the brand of his hand against her back.

Katie gulped. *Now,* she commanded herself.

She clutched her fingers together, as if she could wring some courage from them. "Seth. Well, uh, I should tell you why I wired. I, uh, as you know, I agreed to be a surrogate for Karen and Ryan."

Seth's eyes widened and he went still. Big, solid and still.

The stillness made her babble. "Karen's uterus couldn't maintain a pregnancy, but I'm healthy as a horse and...I wanted to help them *so much.* Karen all but raised me, gave me all the love a little girl needed, and for once, *for once* I could give something back to her."

She backed up against the doorjamb for support. "And...well..."

His intense green gaze pinned her to the spot. "What are you trying to say?"

Katie swallowed, a wash of shivers rolling over her. "I'm trying to tell you I'm going to have a baby."

She watched him carefully. He blinked, like a man just coming to.

"Could you say that again?" His voice sounded quiet and controlled.

"The in vitro worked." She noted with relief the still-neutral expression on his face. This was going to be just fine, she thought. It was disconcerting news, but he seemed to accept it.

"It worked?" he echoed, as if waiting for the words to make sense to him.

"Yes." Katie swallowed through a suddenly tight throat. "I'm pregnant."

Katie's pregnant?

A whirl of emotions washed over Seth. He felt the anguish of his brother's death all over again, quickly followed by a feeling of betrayal. How could Ryan be dead? How could another Cooper male, albeit unintentionally, abandon his child?

Seth put his hands over his eyes, and, breathing heavily, forced the pain away. Minutes passed, and the sounds of the day—cars slipping by, birds chirping—found their way past the *shush* in his ears.

What now? His first instinct was to hit the nearest airport and hightail it to parts unknown. But he couldn't run. Not now.

At least, *not yet.* He had to make sure Katie and the baby—Ryan's baby, he thought, his throat tightening—had a secure future. And he had to get things running smoothly at Ends of the Earth. Then he wouldn't be needed around here anymore. In a few weeks, he would be back on that plane, flying away.

He took his hands from his face. Katie must have some plan in mind. And there was nothing to it but to find out what it was. And where he fit in.

He opened his eyes and swung toward her. Expecting to see her as a pregnant woman now, a *mother,* the jolt the pure beauty of her face gave him came as a surprise. The swing of her blond hair beneath her chin, the wary set of her full-lipped mouth,

her *scent*—God, why was he noticing the sweet fresh-
ness now?—sucker-punched him.

"We need to talk," he said, trying to keep his mind
on the business at hand.

"Yes." Her fingers gripped each other in a tense
bundle.

"A shock," he offered. "The news is just a shock
to me."

She nodded, her head down, her gaze on her white
knuckles. "I know. To me, too, when I first found
out. I hadn't really considered the possibility of being
pregnant, once...once Ryan and Karen died."

Emotion tied his gut in a half hitch. He hadn't even
considered what it would have been like for Katie to
discover she was going to have a parentless baby.
"I'm sorry." He said the worthless phrase, feeling
clumsy.

Her hands relaxed and her head lifted. "Don't be."
The blue honesty of her eyes triggered a footrace of
nerves down his spine. "When I found out about the
baby, I also found a way to be happy again." Her
gaze dropped, hiding her expression from him. "I
don't know if you can understand that."

"Sure," he replied uneasily, then steeled himself
against a premonitory shiver. *Get down to business,
Cooper.* "So, you've been, uh, thinking about it,
then?"

"It?"

"The ba—the pregnancy. What you're going to do

about it.'' She must have some ideas. He could only hope she would go easy explaining them to him.

Her head came up slowly and she focused on him with a laserlike gaze. "What about you? This child is your niece or nephew, the same as it is to me. Are you prepared to be responsible for the baby?"

Seth swallowed hard. His heart started pounding like the clackety-clack of speeding train wheels. *So much for going easy on him.* He could barely hear her over the ringing in his ears.

"Let me tell you what I've been thinking," she continued.

Then she launched into a long speech. Still trying to recover his wits, Seth found himself nodding, over and over.

"Children should have two parents," she said.

He concentrated on bringing air from his nose into his lungs.

"Two parents to care for them. A mother and a father living with them," she went on. "Don't you agree?"

Still attempting to regain a normal breathe-and-swallow rhythm, he didn't answer. To be honest, he didn't have much experience with two-parent households. His father had abandoned the family when he was nine years old and Ryan ten, and the one-parent job his mother had done was uniformly lousy. Worse than lousy.

His silence apparently didn't concern her. She waxed on about her childhood, telling him she'd spent her weeks split between her mother and father. "I don't want that kind of life for this baby." Staring down at her hands, she hesitated, took a breath, then plunged on. "That's where my plan comes in. My, uh, two-parent plan."

Two-parent plan?

Seth's jaw went rock-hard and his hands curled into involuntary fists. She didn't want... She couldn't mean—

"This baby should have a mother *and* father."

Spurred by desperation, he struggled to speak. "But—"

"I'm committed to raising this baby. But not alone."

He heard the dreaded implication as if from a long distance. She wanted him—the consummate bachelor, the man who put continents between himself and commitment—to live with her and raise the baby. A drop of sweat rolled down his temple. He couldn't do it.

She was staring at him as if she could hear every screaming nerve in his body. "What's the matter?"

"It's just that..." He swallowed, trying to ease out the words. "It's just that I'm not sure I'll make a good f—" Hell, he couldn't even say the word.

Her eyebrows pulled together. "A good f—?" she prompted.

"A good f-father."

Her knitted eyebrows flew apart and northward in

easy-to-read astonishment. "You'd make a terrible father!"

His tongue unloosened from the roof of his mouth with a *cluck.* "I would?"

She nodded. "Absolutely. If you always go into cardiac arrest even thinking about it. You're probably lousy husband material, too."

"Well, gee, thanks."

A little laugh escaped her. "You didn't think I meant you, did you?"

"Of course not," he said quickly, still confused, but refusing to let on.

She laughed again. "You did, too."

He crossed his arms over his chest.

She laughed some more. "Let me put you out of your misery, Seth." Another giggle. "You're not part of my plan at all."

She rose from the couch and came close. He looked into her eyes, saw his reflected image looking like a solid mountain of stupidity.

"I want a husband and a father for the baby, all right," she said, the laughter leaving her voice. "And I have someone in mind, Seth." Her hand touched his shoulder. "But it's not you."

2

Touching Seth was the only mistake she'd made, Katie thought. Before that, she'd been doing just fine, explaining about the baby, explaining her plan. Beneath her palm, his shoulder felt solid and warm, like something she wanted to bury her cheek against. But not just that. Below his shoulder was his wide, muscled chest. And it wasn't her cheek she wanted to set against it.

Goose bumps streaked over her skin as a shiver of awareness shot through her. She snatched her hand away. Lord, these extra hormones were dangerous.

His voice rumbled. "If it's not me, then who?"

She stared at him blankly. *Who what?* It took a couple of rushed heartbeats to remember what they'd been talking about. The baby. Her plan. "Yes...yes."

"Who?" he asked again.

Katie tucked her hair nervously behind her ears. "Well, um, there's a man, this nice man I've known a long time, who wants to marry me. He's intelligent, successful. He'd make an excellent father for the baby...."

"Keep going."

Her lips were dry and she licked them. "We've talked around the issue, a little...."

"You and this 'nice' man?"

"Uh-hmm. I haven't said yes—we've just talked generalities, really, because I wanted to talk with you first, as you're the baby's only other relative. But he seems to be everything I want."

His eyebrows rose. "You want marriage with a 'nice' man?"

She didn't like the way he said that. "Well, of course I do. But more than that, he'd be a reliable partner to raise the baby with."

Seth jumped up from the chair. "I don't know." He stared out the front window.

"It could be the perfect answer."

His head turned to look at her, but sunshine streamed through the window, backlighting him, so she couldn't read his expression. "It could be."

Seconds ticked away in silence, then he strode to her. Tucking his knuckle beneath her chin, he lifted her face so she had to meet his eyes. "This is what you want?" he asked softly.

Katie swallowed. How much of his skin was touching hers? Not even a square inch, yet she couldn't think of *what* she wanted. Or maybe what she suddenly wanted she couldn't bear thinking of. "They don't cover this in the pregnancy books," she murmured. They talked about hormone surges, but not about frighteningly strong ones brought on by the totally wrong man.

He grimaced. "I suppose not. And if it's any consolation, I'm as lost as you are."

His misunderstanding didn't lessen the impact of his touch, his presence. She needed to get away from both. "Why don't you leave now. Think about what I've said." She slipped her chin away from his hand and took a step back. "Come to dinner tonight. Tom will be here. Maybe after you've met him..."

"Maybe after I've met him?"

She looked away from his strong shoulders and shaggy, honey-brown hair. Away from his eyes that made her wish— "You'll think it's the best solution, too."

Katie shut the door behind Seth and breathed a huge sigh of relief. He'd agreed to come for dinner tonight, but at least she would have a few hours' respite.

She flopped onto the couch, hugging herself. For the first time since she'd found out she was pregnant, she felt afraid. She'd thought she had the situation under control. But Seth... He complicated everything. Made her doubt her plan.

But darn it, the plan was good. Karen and Ryan had shared her belief in family. They would want that for their baby.

Certainly she could raise the baby alone. She had enough love, but the sense of completeness she'd lacked in her own childhood would then be missing for this child, too.

Probably Seth could be persuaded to take some part in the baby's life, but he'd been obviously stunned by the thought. A person who spent his life wandering wasn't a family man.

Tom Harding defined "family man." Just as she'd told Seth, Tom was intelligent, successful. And he wanted her, and seemed to want a family. He would be the male balance in her baby's life. A man who would stick by her forever.

Marrying Tom solved everything.

Katie rose from the couch with determination and headed toward the kitchen, blocking out the memory of her last glimpse of Seth's face and his skeptical expression.

So what? At dinner tonight she would dispel any doubts Seth might have...and all the rest of hers.

Seth rubbed his gritty eyes and stared at the paper-clip-and-coffee-cup remains of the afternoon's meeting at the San Francisco headquarters of Ends of the Earth. He swiveled his chair toward the only attendee left, his brother's trusted assistant, Grace. "It's a mess, isn't it?" he asked.

Her sympathetic expression didn't waver. "Ends of the Earth can't run itself."

"I thought maybe Phyllis, or Jared..."

Grace was already shaking her head. "Not yet,

anyway. It will take some time. Probably a lot of time.''

In six or seven months the baby will be born. He couldn't suppress the thought, or the curious ache it brought.

''I wanted to be gone in a few weeks,'' he said, shrugging off the feeling. ''At the outside.''

Grace pursed her lips. ''There are others in the field who can take over your job. We need you here. For all those years you let Ryan call the shots, Seth. But the company's your baby now.''

He winced. *Bad choice of words.* And Grace thought he should stick around and take over Ryan's duties. The conference-room walls seemed to close in on him. Maybe she was wrong. Maybe he could train Phyllis *and* Jared to do Ryan's job, and train them quickly if he put all his time into it.

He rolled his chair away from the conference table. Once he resolved the situation with Katie, he could concentrate fully on the business. Tonight he would put that problem to rest and then move back to what needed to be done at Ends of the Earth. And then, finally, he would take himself away, back *to* the ends of the earth.

Seth knocked at Katie's door that evening. A roundly pregnant young woman with Lucy Ricardo curls and a clashing sense of color answered. Seth smiled at her and her red-checked top and purple pants, determined to like everyone and everything this evening. Getting Katie settled with a plan and a man meant *his* life could get back to normal.

The woman had a strong grip and a friendly grin. "I'm Izzy," she said. "I think you know my husband, Dan, and I'm also Katie's partner in the candy biz. She's barfing, by the way."

Seth blinked. "How...unpleasant. Should I come back?"

"Naw." Izzy shook her head and the corkscrew curls glinted in the last of the afternoon light. "Come into the kitchen. She's probably better by now." As Izzy led the way, she tossed a last remark over her shoulder. "And Tom's here."

Tom. Seth had only a second to reabsorb the "nice man's" name before he was shaking the nice man's hand. "Tom Harding," the guy said. "Pleased to meet you."

Tom Harding was a thirtyish blond man who could be a banker, a stockbroker, or a software executive—any one of a number of no-recession-will-touch-me types who strode up Market Street in San Francisco or dressed down on Fridays in the Silicon Valley. He wore a pair of overstarched khakis and a blue oxford-cloth shirt and within minutes told Seth he was head honcho at a financial-software firm.

Can I call 'em, or what? Seth thought.

Mr. Success was telling Seth about the homemade artichoke-crab dip and the cheesecake he'd brought over when a wan-looking Katie walked into the kitchen. Tom, obviously a sensitive type, kissed her gently on the forehead. Seth sketched a wave as she dropped into a kitchen chair.

"Hello, Seth." She'd changed into a soft-looking tunic-and-tights outfit. Her lips, tinted a pale pink, curved up. He couldn't stop his gaze from running down to her still-flat abdomen. Something primitive inside him sparked, and he stamped out the flames.

"You've been sick?" he asked. Kind of indelicate, he knew, but Tom was shoving crackers and his "homemade" dip under her nose and maybe somebody needed to point out that she might not want it there.

"Mmm-hmm. First time. But now I'm starving." She dug into the dip with obvious relish. Tom wore an indulgent smirk on his successful face.

Seth began to realize he didn't have an instantaneous like for the guy.

"Wonderful, Tom. I can't believe you rushed home after a full day and made this. A cheesecake, too!"

Seth didn't believe it, either. He tasted the dip himself, and it was excellent. He suspected Tom had a cook, even when the guy began listing the FBI-level secrets to his cheesecake.

"Katie, where are the onions?" Izzy interrupted.

"Lower shelf of the pantry." Katie sighed. "I should get up and help you."

Izzy shook her head. "Stay put. You're letting me sponge dinner since Dan's out tonight. The least I can do is make pasta sauce when you don't feel well."

"I have a great pasta recipe," Tom began. "Why don't you let me—"

"I'll do mine," Seth found himself saying.

Mr. Success's gaze flicked over Seth. "*You* cook?"

The man's disbelief struck Seth as a compliment. "Yes," he said, although he had never made anything fancier than a burger or a grilled-cheese sandwich in his life. But how hard could it be? He'd eaten pasta hundreds, no, thousands of times.

He liked the look of pleased surprise on Katie's face. A hint of pink warmed her country-club cheekbones. "Wow," she said softly. "I'd love to taste yours."

He grinned. "I'll take that in the cleanest way possible," he said, then laughed at the stunned expressions on both her face and Tom's. Behind him, Izzy giggled, and then Katie joined in, her face pinkening even more. He liked it. He liked Katie's pink face, her laugh and the disgruntled look that Mr. Success gave him.

He stopped himself from swaggering toward the refrigerator by remembering he didn't know what the hell he was doing. "What first?" Izzy asked.

"Boil the pasta," he directed. He didn't know how much or for how long, but his bluff seemed to work because Izzy began bustling around the kitchen.

He opened the refrigerator and stared inside, listening to Tom telling Katie about all the grand decisions he'd made that day. When she tried to tell him about a problem with her work, he immediately interrupted.

When she mentioned something about her pregnancy, he changed the subject altogether.

Seth continued staring into the fridge. *What went in pasta sauce, anyway?* He pulled out tomatoes, celery, mushrooms, bean sprouts, and some other stuff. Izzy appeared beside him, and with a conspiratorial smile, returned the sprouts and the red apples and pointed him toward the butcher block. Now he stared at the items jumbled on the hardwood. What should he do now? Maybe a blender... Or should he just put them in a pan and smush them around with a spoon?

"Here's the butcher knife," Izzy said. "Do you use tomato sauce and then add this other stuff to it?" She winked.

Seth hadn't traveled all over the world for nothing. He knew when a gift was handed to him on a silver platter. "Yes," he answered. "Exactly."

The awkward thumps of his knife against the wooden block punctuated the conversation between Katie and Tom.

"We've got to be in Tahoe next winter," he was saying. "We're talking about a corporate team-building ski vacation. You'll love it there, Katie."

"I'm sure I would, but..." Her gaze flicked down to her abdomen. Seth knew she was thinking about the baby. "You know, by then..."

An irritated expression crossed Tom's too-good-looking face. "That's what nannies are for, Katie. So parents can get a break." He paused, obviously thinking. "But taking the baby along could be useful, too—with the nanny, of course."

Katie smiled at the guy like he'd discovered penicillin. "I'd like to have the baby with us," she said softly.

Seth had an urge to shout *Over my dead body,* but he suppressed it, instead chopping vigorously at a cauliflower head the bland color of Tom's hair.

"Might look good to come as a family," Tom continued, his fingers drumming against his chin. "Jack Evans, the CEO, is a devoted grandfather."

Seth rolled his eyes, dissecting the cauliflower's brains. But as Izzy helped him with the rest of the meal and as they sat down to eat it, Seth made himself give Tom a break. The guy was handsome, he cooked, and he even politely professed to like the cauliflower Seth had inadvertently added to the sauce instead of the salad.

And, no surprise, Tom did dishes. Seth busied himself about the kitchen, pretending to help.

Hands buried in suds, Tom caught Seth's eye. "So," he said heartily. "You're the absentee uncle."

Seth froze, his fist squeezing the handful of silverware he carried. *Absentee uncle.* It suddenly hit him that if Katie married, he probably would be out of the baby's life for the most part. Out of Katie's life. He swallowed, forced himself to relax his hold. "So you want to be a father to the baby."

There was the briefest of hesitations. "Katie and I haven't firmed our plans quite yet. I knew her years ago when we went to college in L.A. We dated for some time before I took a job here. When she moved this way to open Katie's Candies, *she* called *me*." A smug smile broke over his face.

Well, whoop-de-do. "I suppose since she didn't know a soul besides her sister and my brother it makes a bit of sense...." Seth noted with satisfaction that the other man's smile faltered, then died.

Tom didn't try to buddy him up after that. Seth was glad for it, and even gladder when Mr. Success announced he had to leave.

What, gotta get home to starch your personality— I mean, pants? Seth thought.

Izzy asked to bum a ride home from Tom and they both left.

Seth settled determinedly at the kitchen table with a full mug of hot coffee. Across from him, Katie sipped hesitantly at some herbal-smelling tea.

A little of the tension left his body and he stretched his legs in front of him. His ankle brushed her calf, but he didn't pull away. He watched the steam from her cup rise up to kiss her cheeks, and let a strange feeling of connection to her travel up his leg like pin-pricks of pleasure-pain.

"So, uh, what did you think of Tom?" She didn't look up, as if she was prepared to check his answer against that in her tea leaves.

Absentee uncle. Seth couldn't get those words out of his head. God knew they were likely true, but this situation was more complicated than branches on a family tree. Katie had agreed to do his brother a monumental good turn and he was beginning to feel like he owed her one in return.

Damn it.

He felt her blue-laser eyes on him again. "Did you like him?" she asked.

"I wanted to," Seth said honestly. "And..." Here was where *his* good deed could come in.

"And?" Her pink lips pursed and warm color tinged her cheeks. He knew she held her breath.

"What's not to like?" he said, then closed his mouth, although every instinct he owned shouted *Everything!*

Katie let herself into the kitchen of Katie's Candies and immediately collapsed onto the floral love seat occupying one corner. Closing her eyes and leaning her head back, she spoke to Izzy, who was boxing chocolates at the long counter.

"You won't believe it," Katie said. "*I* hardly believe it." Her voice was hoarse and her throat tight.

Izzy pushed off her disposable gloves and rushed toward Katie. "What? Is something wrong with the baby? Are you okay?"

Izzy's hands clasped hers, warm against Katie's icy fingers. "Well, the doctor was still a little miffed that I'd canceled my appointments after Ryan and Karen's accident. But the babies are fine. I'm not sure *I'm* over the shock."

The play of expressions over Izzy's face would

probably be a comical memory in about eighteen years. Concern, relief, puzzlement. Suddenly her eyes rounded and her throat worked. "Did you say *babies?*"

Katie held up her fingers. "*V* as in *victory*. Two." The sting of tears came to her eyes and she swiped at them with the back of her hand. "I don't know if I'm doubly happy or doubly scared."

Izzy smiled. "How about some of both?"

In unspoken agreement, they leaned toward each other and hugged. Katie felt another hot tear spill onto her cheek. "Ryan and Karen would be so happy."

Izzy leaned back and patted her hand. "And now you have two nieces, or two nephews, or maybe, one of—"

"They're mine," Katie said emphatically. "Ryan and Karen are gone, and now I'm the mommy. They would want that. *I* want that."

"I know." A sudden smile brightened Izzy's face. "You'll have to join one of those mommy-of-twins clubs."

Katie didn't feel quite as cheerful. "But what about a daddy?"

Izzy's expression neutralized. "I thought you had good ol' Tom pegged for that role."

"I'm not sure Seth approves. He said he liked Tom, but when I asked for a go-ahead, he asked for a few days to think about it."

"So?" Izzy's eyebrows rose.

"So Ryan felt very close to Seth. I want him to think I've made the right choice."

"Do you have doubts?" Izzy asked.

Katie shrugged and avoided the question. "I'm sure once I tell Tom and Seth about the twins, we'll work the arrangements out quickly. I need to think about the babies now."

Izzy nodded in understanding.

"Babies." Katie couldn't stop the smile creeping over her face. "Twins," she whispered to herself. Her palm smoothed over her abdomen. *I'll get you both a daddy and we'll be one happy family.*

Seth accepted his second invitation to dinner at Katie's in the space of two days. His secretary had taken the call, and she'd also phoned back his acceptance for him.

On Katie's doorstep, he raked his hands through his hair. After a fourteen-hour day, he needed coffee. But once inside, Izzy shoved a sweating bottle of beer into his palm instead. A lime-green bow scrunched her wild hair to the side. "To ease the pain," she said, and winked.

The pain? Then Katie entered the living room and he thought he knew what Izzy meant. He took the impact of her shining hair and tentative-but-welcoming smile like a blow to the chest.

Tom Harding will have himself a beautiful bride.

Seth focused on the thought to cool the strange burning in his blood. The marriage was a good idea, of course. In the gray hours of early morning he'd realized that holding out approval of Katie's plan to marry the other man had merely been a weird, uncharacteristic reaction on his part.

Most likely brought on by the overseas flight. Call it "reality lag."

If Katie wanted Tom, she should have him.

Still staring at her, Seth rose from his chair. "Could I talk to you a minute?" He shot a look at the ever-interested Izzy. "Alone?"

Why wait? Instead of sitting through dinner, he could tell Katie right now he didn't mind her marriage, didn't object to Tom adopting Ryan and Karen's baby. Then he could go back to the office and get in a couple more hours of work.

Katie licked her lips. "Uh…sure." She gestured vaguely toward the kitchen and then led off in that direction.

The doorbell rang, halting her movement down the hall. She started nervously. "That'll be Tom," she said.

Izzy called out that she would answer the door, but Katie acted like she didn't hear and whipped around, her shoulder brushing Seth's biceps. "I need to get him a drink," she explained, and edged past Seth to head back to the living room.

Seth rubbed at his tingling arm as he followed her. *Fine, she can greet her guest, her* fiancé, *then I'll drag her to the kitchen, say her marriage plans are all right with me, and split.*

But one glimpse of the other guy's perfectly trimmed hair and obvious, fresh shave put Seth's teeth on edge. He traced the stubble on his own jaw as he watched Katie's fingers brush Tom's when she handed him a glass of Chardonnay. *To hell with it*.

He could walk out of her life after dinner.

The meal was even stranger than the day before's. Although Katie served a mouthwatering roasted chicken, she ate almost nothing, said nearly nothing, and stared absently at nothing at all. Izzy volunteered for dish duty and Katie roused herself enough to insist the men join her in the living room over cups of coffee.

Seth was getting antsy. Mounds of work waited in his office—Ryan's office, actually—and the less-than-five weeks until the fateful board of directors meeting suddenly didn't seem nearly enough time. With the exception of *his* exception to being the "absentee" uncle—he wanted to clear up that small issue—he didn't have any business with these two.

He gulped down his coffee and slapped his palms against his thighs. "I oughta be going." He gave Katie a small salute. "Can I give you a quick call tomorrow?"

She just stared at him, her mouth working. "I went to the doctor today," she finally blurted out.

At the anxious expression on her face, Seth sat back down. Now Tom popped up. "I've got to go myself," he said.

"I went to the doctor today," Katie said again.

Tom's lips quirked in a half smile. "Yes, well. I'm sure it's a private matter and I've got to get home."

Katie paled. "But—"

Tom interrupted. "I'll call you—"

"Sit down," Seth ordered.

Tom sat.

"We're listening, Katie. You went to the doctor today." Seth put on a reassuring smile, although his heart was clattering at the worry in Katie's eyes. "Is everything all right?"

A tremulous smile broke over her face. "Well, I think so. Um. Uh. I'm carrying twins. Two healthy babies."

The word *"healthy"* calmed his pulse. The words *"twins"* and *"two"* took a few seconds to sink in. "Wow," he said.

"Whoa," Tom said.

Seth's gaze swung toward Tom. He was standing again, his feet doing a backward shuffle toward the door. *"Two?"* he asked.

Seth glanced at Katie's fading smile. "Sit down," he told the other man.

Tom sat.

Seth cleared his throat. "So you have two healthy babies. That's great."

"Two healthy babies," Tom echoed. "Two babies. Two."

Seth tried ignoring the shock and near distaste in the guy's voice and directed his comments to Katie. "Well, there you go. A ready-made family."

Tom started echoing again. "Ready-made family." He stood, shaking his head. "Two. I can't do two."

"Sit—"

Seth stopped, because now Katie was standing as well.

Her voice was quiet, calm. "What are you trying to say, Tom?"

"I thought I could do it. I thought I could take on another man's child and make it my own." He started shaking his head again. "But *two*. That's an entire family."

"Yes." Katie nodded.

"But I don't think it would ever feel like *my* family."

Seth watched Katie swallow. He followed the deliberate movement with his eyes, the muscles in her throat working beneath now pink skin.

"I understand," she said.

Seth started to get worried. "Now, wait just a minute..."

Tom had the back shuffle down and was almost at the front door.

Katie made a gesture with her hand, cutting him off. "This is goodbye, isn't it, Tom?"

Seth got to his feet. "What do you mean, goodbye? What kind of man walks out on a woman at a time like this?"

The other two acted as if they didn't hear him.

Tom gave another half smile, his hand on the doorknob. "Good luck, Katie."

"Take care of yourself, Tom."

The civility made Seth nuts. "What the hell—"

The door clicked shut behind Tom.

His mouth open, Seth swung toward Katie. "What the hell—" he started again.

"The hell of it is," Katie said calmly, "now I don't have a daddy for the babies."

3

←→←

A chill dropped over Katie, like a sheet over a ghostly Halloween trick-or-treater. Wrapping her arms around herself, she turned away from Seth.

Her fingers bit into her arms. She'd felt numb when Karen and Ryan died, then rejuvenated by the news of her pregnancy. Then, content with the idea of Tom as a partner in raising the children.

But now, with that partnership dissolved before it began, loneliness and worry had found her.

"Katie, you okay?" Concern filled Seth's voice.

She still didn't face him, afraid tears would spill over if she moved. She didn't want him to see her cry. As a matter of fact, she didn't want him to see her at all—ever.

"I'm fine." Amazing how calm her voice sounded. "You can go home." On some purely female level, she was humiliated that he'd witnessed Tom's rejection of her.

"I don't want to leave you alone."

Katie closed her eyes at the last word. But she was

on her own now, and might as well get used to it. "I'm not. Izzy's here."

As if on cue, Izzy breezed into the living room, her purse in one hand, her other palm cupped over her belly. "G'night, guys, I'm going home. Darn Braxton Hicks." She rubbed her round tummy. "Giving me fits." The front door closed firmly behind her.

Katie could have stopped her with a word, but she was too tired for anyone at the moment. Now she just had to send Seth on his way.

"Braxton Hicks?"

Seth's voice sounded so appalled that Katie reluctantly swung his way.

"Dan and Izzy are naming their baby *Braxton Hicks?*"

Seth was relieved that Katie was finally looking at him, even more relieved when a reluctant smile washed the bleakness from her face.

"Silly," she said. "Pregnant women have practice contractions, especially in the third trimester. They're called Braxton Hicks."

"Oh." There was a lot to know about pregnancy. Trimesters. Contractions. *Braxton Hicks.*

"You can leave now, Seth." Like the vision of an inviting oasis in the desert, Katie's smile dissolved. "I'll be fine by myself."

By herself. Seth raked his fingers through his hair. She was going to be alone tonight, through the pregnancy, while raising the children. His brother's children. Seth's own nieces or nephews.

His hands fisted, and he hid them in the pockets of his khakis. "But... How are you going to do it?"

She shrugged and didn't pretend to misunderstand him. "One day at a time. Then one feeding at a time, I suppose." Her hands flapped in his direction. "Don't you worry about it. Go on home."

Seth took a step toward the door. He *should* get home. Well, back to the office, actually. Every minute he spent there underscored how right his brother's assistant Grace was. He wasn't going to be wandering again. Not for a long while, anyway. With Ryan gone, the company needed him.

"Goodb—" He glanced over at Katie and his mouth dried. She was somewhere else, her glittering sapphire eyes blank. Reliving Tom's farewell? Imagining the future, when her belly grew round with the babies?

A fingernail tickle of some strange sensation trailed down his spine. He took another step toward the door. "Good—" Then his own words slammed into his head, the words he'd said to Tom. *What do you mean, goodbye? What kind of man walks out on a woman at a time like this?*

"Katie." He hardly recognized the urgency in his own voice. She didn't respond, obviously still caught in her own thoughts. "Katie," he said again. "Listen to me."

She came to awareness slowly, as she might come awake from sleep, he thought. He banished the vision of her warm skin on cool cotton sheets.

"Go home, Seth," she said.

With Ryan gone, the company needed him. With Ryan gone, didn't Ryan's children need him, as well? He knew, in excruciating, firsthand detail, how it felt to be fatherless.

"Not yet." A little hum started in Seth's ears, and he felt the adrenaline sluicing through him; ideas, images, darting through his mind with brilliant intensity, like that night in a Naples alley when he'd faced a mugger with a flashing knife.

The irony made him grimace. Like that night, his life was on the line. "Maybe we have something else to discuss."

She sighed. "Not tonight, Seth."

"Yes, tonight." Before he wimped out. Before he convinced himself he didn't need to do the right thing. He took a breath and spoke over that adrenaline buzz. "Marry me, Katie."

"I—" She stopped, as if his words finally sank in.

"Won't? Can't? Want to?" Seth strode toward her. "Just say you will."

She still looked stunned.

He couldn't resist touching the golden curve of her hair. He slid his fingers through it, just brushing against the silky skin of her cheek, and then tucked the strands behind her ear.

She shivered. "I—I don't understand."

The buzz in his ears was pitched higher, now that he'd touched her. "It doesn't have to be a conventional marriage, but this isn't a conventional situation. I'll do my best as a father, though.''

"But, but…'' Her hand gestured vaguely. "You're… You won't be around. You're always off on some adventure for the company's sake. You… You wander.''

"I did. But Ends of the Earth needs me here. There's a meeting with the board in about five weeks, and I'm certain they're going to insist I stay and run the company.''

She was hugging herself again, her face vulnerable, with huge eyes and pink-flushed cheeks. "Marriage to Tom seemed safe and sane.''

Seth held out his arms. "No traffic violations since I got back to the States. No crazy Aunt Hepzibah locked in the attic.''

Katie shook her head. "Maybe somebody'd better lock *me* in the attic. And didn't you just get back to the States two days ago?''

"See?'' Seth couldn't believe how important it was that she say yes. "And still no speeding tickets. It may be a personal record.''

He saw some of the tension had left her body at his teasing. *Good.* Without a doubt, if the tables were turned, Ryan would do this for him. And Seth didn't want to do any less for Ryan. Maybe she would want to end their arrangement someday, but she would have his support now when she needed it, and the babies would have a father.

Katie bit her lip. "Karen and Ryan—''

"Would want two parents for the babies. Didn't you tell me that yourself?"

He knew he'd convinced her. The air in the room warmed, and she swayed toward him, almost imperceptibly. But he sensed it, and finally adrenaline gave its final push, making him do what he'd wanted to do since the moment he'd seen her again.

He pulled her gently into his arms. Held her loosely, so she wouldn't get scared. He remembered again their dance at Ryan's wedding—the scent of her perfume, the sweet softness of her hair against his chin. "What do you say, Katie?"

Katie's mind reeled. To feel so lonely and then to have Seth offer marriage. The warmth of his arms was sweet—but scary too. She pulled back and stared into his eyes. Was it too easy an answer? Too soon?

Concern for her filled his gaze. Concern for hers, the babies. They were his flesh and blood too. His big hand moved against her back, offering comfort and protection. All that she wanted in a father for the babies. In a husband. She took a blind leap. "Yes," she whispered, hopefulness and optimism blossoming around her heart. "I say yes."

Katie stood across the room from Seth, still surprised by...*everything*. Twins, no Tom, marriage to Seth.

She'd carefully stepped away from his embrace the moment she'd agreed, and now they'd spent several moments in awkward silence.

But she didn't feel alone anymore. Or vulnerable.

Not with the shaggy-haired Seth looming in her living room like an unbending column of strength. She touched her abdomen, imagining the two tiny hearts beating underneath her skin. *A daddy.*

From somewhere—from the two little sweethearts inside her, she guessed—came a wide yawn. She clapped her hand over her mouth. Sleepiness at a time like this?

Seth came toward her. "You're tired. Now I really *should* go."

She half smiled. "Sorry. I..." *I'm glad you're leaving before I can do or say anything else impetuous.* Not that she wanted to take back her agreement. Not that.

"I understand." His fingers lightly brushed her cheek.

Not that either! When he touched her, all sorts of impetuous, *un*pregnant things came to mind. His knuckles stroked her again, and the sensation relayed straight to her stomach, thanks to Olympic-speed nerve impulses. She felt nervous, giddy. *Womanly.*

She sidestepped toward the door. "Good night, then."

He followed.

At the doorway she hesitated, unsure if she should pull it open—would that look like she was trying to get rid of him?—or... She glanced over her shoulder to read his expression.

Her thought flow halted. His green eyes stared intently at her face, and it took a minute to shake herself free of them. "Good night," she said again, a little desperately, as if the finality of the word could stop her from admiring the wide strength of his shoulders, the glint of gold in the evening stubble on his chin, the unbearable fascination of his chiseled mouth.

"Good night," he murmured back, the words automatically spoken, the leaning of his body toward hers anything but automatic. His hand grasped her shoulder—nerve impulses started that crazy race again—and gently, firmly, turned her around. His head lowered.

She saw his eyes, chin, eyes again, and then she couldn't look away from his mouth. Closer, it was the ruddy pink of a man's mouth; closer, and her eyes shut, and a gentle, smooth touch glided over her lips.

Somebody made a little sound. *Oh, no, it was me.* The glide again, and then he came back a third time with firm pressure.

Those racing nerve impulses shrieked with glee, sending the message all around—stomach, heart, knees—that this was a good kiss. A great kiss. An awesome kiss.

She opened her mouth because the pressure insisted and because she wanted to, and she tasted his tongue. He pushed it firmly into her mouth and stroked.

Shivers ran down Katie's arms. With each hand, she pinched a bit of his shirt, afraid to grab on to him, but afraid she would fall down without some support.

He lifted his mouth, and she instantly released that

small hold she had on him. His cheek scratched hers and his harsh breath rasped in her ear.

More shivers. Another job for those overworked nerves of hers.

She heard him swallow.

And again.

Then his voice came out, rough. "Good night."

She had to smile, although her common sense was taking over from the nerves and was jumping up and down in warning. Seth sounded so...overwhelmed. "See you later."

He inhaled a huge breath, then shifted away from her. His eyes were darker, his chest still moving heavily. "I...uh..." His hand gestured vaguely between the two of them. "I don't exactly know..."

She found the guts to pat him on the shoulder. "I do," she said reassuringly.

His eyebrows rose.

"Hormones," she said with conviction. "Pregnant women have way more than their fair share."

He blinked, nodded as if he was filing the fact away, and opened the front door. Katie closed it behind him.

Whew. He hadn't noticed.

She leaned her back against the door to help out her still-wobbly knees. While hormones might explain *her* impetuous reaction to the kiss, it did nothing at all to explain *his*.

In a daze, Katie walked out of the thoroughly modern and totally unromantic San Mateo County courthouse as the new Mrs. Seth Cooper. Her wedding band still felt hot, as it had the minute it left Seth's breast pocket for the cold tremble of her hand.

The past thirty minutes had seemed like one of those topsy-turvy dreams, where you found yourself at work in your pajamas or on a desperately important errand without directions.

There was no map for this kind of marriage.

To underscore the strangeness of it all, her shoulder merely brushed Seth's arm as they walked, while it was Izzy who clutched her hand.

"I'm so excited," Izzy said, her orange hair confined in a yellow snood, her fingers squeezing Katie's new ring so it bit into her hand. "But are you sure you shouldn't have called your mother and your father?"

Katie shook her head. She would send them each a letter tomorrow. They hadn't concerned themselves with her for years, except as a way to hurt each other. "There wasn't enough time," she said. Seth had insisted the wedding take place as soon as the waiting period allowed.

They all stopped on the wide sidewalk outside the courthouse, waiting for the only other witness, Dan, to bring Seth's car around from the metered lot.

Izzy grinned. "The eager bridegroom," she said, gazing at Seth with satisfaction.

Katie sent her friend a quelling look. She guessed eagerness wasn't Seth's impetus for a quick wedding.

Unless it was eagerness to get the whole ordeal over with.

For reassurance, she put her hand on her abdomen. *We're doing this for you.* She'd told herself that time and again over the past few days and had felt comforted by the thought.

Seth apparently noticed the gesture. For the first time that day he voluntarily touched her, running his hand down the back of her hair. "You feeling okay?"

Katie smiled. "I'm fine." His gaze met hers and the memory of their lips touching was clear in his eyes. She hastily looked down the street. She'd also warned herself time and again in the preceding days that this shaky arrangement with Seth didn't need passion in the mix.

Seth's Explorer rounded the corner and Izzy stepped between Katie and Seth to link one arm with each of them. "Let's go to our house for a party! A celebration!"

Celebration? Katie thought. She slid a glance at Seth and he looked as startled as she at the idea.

"No, Izzy," she said quickly.

"I insist," Izzy said, pushing them toward the car now halted at the curb. "You have to take Dan and me home anyway."

Dan leaned over to open a passenger door. "The Nuptial Express! Bound for Dan and Izzy's! All aboard!"

Katie had to smile at Dan's infectious good humor.

Even Seth looked less brooding. Maybe if they spent the evening with Dan and Izzy, this newlywed daze—okay, call it like it was, *awkwardness*—would ease.

As the car wound its way along the coastal mountain road toward Dan and Izzy's remote house, Seth buried the tension of the new marriage as he'd buried every concern he'd had about it for the past four days—deeply and quickly. For now, he would try to forget about the marriage altogether. Yeah, he would just pretend he was having an evening out with friends.

In the back seat, Seth left several inches of space between himself and Katie. She looked beautiful, as always—her blond hair curving around her face, a loose, off-white dress draping her slender frame.

He hadn't seen her since his proposal. Overwhelmed with work, he'd only made time for daily afternoon phone calls. "How's it going?" he would ask. Subtext: *Have you changed your mind?* She would reply, "Okay. Good." Her subtext: *I'm willing if you're willing.*

So they'd gone through with it. And it was going to be just fine. He would learn to be a father and— He squashed the burgeoning worry. Just a guy out for the evening with friends, remember?

Izzy turned around in the front seat to face them, a smile bisecting the sea of freckles on her face. She looked at Katie. "So, if not your folks, is there *any-one* you told about your wedding?"

So much for forgetting about the marriage.

Katie frowned. "Don't make it sound like I'm trying to hide it. I spoke to Tom yesterday over the phone. He knows."

"Tom?" Seth spat the other man's name from his mouth. "What the hell would you call him for?"

Katie stared out the window. "I didn't call him. He called me."

A spurt of heat burned in Seth's gut. "Why?"

She shrugged.

He narrowed his eyes. "He didn't have second thoughts, did he? He didn't change his mind and propose again?"

Katie looked at him now, an expression in her blue eyes that annoyed him. "What kind of person do you think I am?" There was a jittery edge to her voice. "If he had, I would have let you off the hook."

"That's not what I mean!" Another flame of anger kindled in the pit of his belly. Now that they were married, he didn't want to think of Katie as someone else's wife. Especially not that jerk's.

"What did you mean?" Katie asked.

Izzy's eyebrows rose in twin rusty arches. "Yeah, so what *did* you mean?"

Dan saved Seth from answering. "We're here!" he called, the car's tires spitting gravel as he braked in the drive.

A tissue-paper bell hung from the porch beam of

Dan and Izzy's rustic cottage. Congratulations!—spelled out in silver—curved on a banner over the front door.

Inside was a well-laid fire, two bottles of sparkling cider, a bottle of good champagne, and a small, two-tiered cake topped with a plastic dancing bride and groom.

Seth guessed that they would at least have to toast before they talked of something other than the marriage.

He was right. Within moments, the fire roared, the champagne bubbled in the flute in his hand, and Dan made a goofy speech about the future and wedded bliss. He ended it with a wink.

Seth knocked back his entire glass in one gulp and refused to feed Katie a piece of cake. She looked relieved.

"You guys are no fun," Izzy complained.

Seth tried to get off the subject of weddings by asking Dan about his opinion of the NFL season. Over Dan's enthusiastic assessment, came Katie's laughing voice.

"No fun? Just no fools," she was saying to Izzy. "I've been there, done that, remember?"

Been there, done that? Seth tuned out Dan's long-winded bemoaning of Joe Montana's retirement and how the 49ers would never be the same, to listen to the two women.

"You're only mad because you got some icing in

your hair that time," Izzy said, then laughed. "Brad called you the Icing Queen instead of the Ice Queen."

Brad?

"Ha-ha. And I got icing everywhere. In my hair, on the flowers—I bet there's even some on the marriage certificate."

Dan droned on about the passing defense and the lousy Monday-night football schedule but Seth couldn't listen. Had Katie been married before? It sure sounded like it. And Brad? Who was Brad?

Izzy laughed again and took a sip of the sparkling cider she and Katie were drinking. "I remember Brad volunteering to lick it all off."

Seth couldn't take it anymore. "What are you talking about? *Who* are you talking about?"

Except Dan answered. "Football." He blinked. "You asked me, remember? And Montana." He sighed. "The game'll never be the same without Montana...."

Seth groaned inwardly and stopped listening to Dan again. But the women had hopscotched to a new chocolate recipe they were working on. He looked back to his buddy. "Who's Brad?" he asked abruptly.

Dan halted, his mouth mid-Montana moan. "Brad?" His brows came together. "Offense? Defense?"

Seth ground his teeth and lowered his voice. "That's what I'm trying to find out. *Katie's* Brad. And he sounds pretty offensive to me." Lick it off. Damn.

Dan's brow cleared. "Oh, that's an old bf—boy-friend—of Katie's. I think she was engaged to him for a while maybe." He gestured vaguely. "But then he went somewhere."

"Brad's a medical missionary in India." Katie's voice came from across the room, cool and noncommittal.

A wave of embarrassment heated Seth's neck.

Izzy sighed. "We all loved Brad. We were talking about a little cake-throwing debacle at Dan's and my wedding. Katie stepped in to stop a couple of over-indulging guests from destroying our cake and kind of got, uh, smeared."

Seth's neck-heat didn't subside and he couldn't get past the first sentence. *We all loved Brad.* Did that mean Katie, too?

He looked at her as she stared into her crystal flute, a funny, sad little smile on her face.

Suddenly the force of what he'd done this afternoon rose like a zombie from the place he'd buried it. He was married. To someone who had Toms and Brads in her past. Who had memories that made her smile sadly.

She's a stranger. The weirdness of that thought pounded at his brain.

Brad. Tom. Lick it off.

And so far, what he'd found out he didn't know about her, he didn't like at all.

If that made any sense.

* * *

Katie settled herself into the front seat of Seth's car and rested her head against the seat back.

In the dashboard glow, Seth gave her a little smile. "Tired?" he asked.

"A little." They'd stayed at Dan and Izzy's house until well after dark.

"Are you sure you know the way back?" she asked. She'd noticed that Seth had only drunk that first glass of champagne hours ago, so she wasn't worried about him driving home.

"There's just the one road, right?"

She nodded. "And problems galore when it washes out with a big storm. Happens at least a couple of times a year. Dan and Izzy were stuck for a long weekend here about seven months ago." She paused. "As in Izzy is seven months pregnant."

Seth's teeth flashed in the darkness. "Do I detect an eerie coincidence?"

Katie laughed and closed her eyes as they turned from the driveway onto the road. "Eerie? Let's just say the house will always hold a special spot in Dan's and Izzy's hearts."

Katie sighed, thinking of Dan and Izzy to block her own unsettled emotions. In the warm darkness of the car, she smiled, remembering the wedding cake and sparkling cider.

Heat from the car's vents basted her toes. Something about Dan's toast and wink had ignited a small worry at the back of her mind. She yawned. Something she'd forgotten to take care of, or... The niggle wouldn't go away. What was it...? She yawned again.

The car lurched, and Katie came to fuzzy-headed wakefulness. Her body angled awkwardly and her cheek rested on the heavy strength of...of...a man's thigh.

She started to jerk away, then felt a familiar touch on her hair. "Sorry, Sleeping Beauty. I hit a pothole. Go back to sleep."

Seth. Somehow she'd ended up sleeping in Seth's lap.

His palm continued to stroke her hair, but despite his soothing touch, she sat up. Her gaze leaped to the steering wheel and his left hand, where the ring she'd placed on it that afternoon gleamed dully in the meager light. No, she hadn't dreamed it. She and Seth were married.

He shot her a look. "We're almost there. You okay, Beauty?"

She half smiled at the silly nickname. "I'm okay. Just ready for be—" And then that little niggle from before became a full-force nag.

Marriage. Husband. Bed.

4

▬◄▬

Parked outside Katie's darkened house, Seth sat in the car without moving. She didn't seem any more inclined than he to leave the vehicle's warm, neutral haven. After another moment's stillness, he worried that something was wrong.

He ran a thumb down the side of her cheek. Reassured by its warmth and the quick catch of her breath, he allowed himself one more slow stroke.

"Thank you," she said.

For the touch?

"For your support," she added quickly. "For putting up with Izzy and Dan's celebration."

He groaned. "And I'll thank you to remind me never to bring up the 49ers to Dan again. Ever."

Her smile flashed in the darkness. "He is... passionate." Then, as if trying to escape the last word, she nearly dived out of the car.

To keep up with her, Seth moved quickly too, stopping first to grab his luggage from the back, then following her hurried footsteps up the front walk.

It was her front door that halted him. Not the fact

that it was locked—"I have a key for you inside," she'd said—not the fact that he couldn't open it for Katie because his hand gripped the straps of his leather backpack and equally worn duffel.

No, the front door stopped him cold because it had a *threshold.*

And he was a groom and she was a bride and they were married.

Panic grabbed him around the throat and squeezed. He dropped the bags.

She fumbled in her purse for her keys, buying Seth a few more minutes.

What to do? Tradition had no place in this marriage. They were strangers, forced into a situation for the sake of the babies. The only thing they had in common was a family tree and an obligation.

She found the key, turned it in the lock, and the door swung open. Panic squeezed again. *What to do?*

As if she heard his bewilderment, Katie looked at him. In the porch light, violet, sleep-needy shadows showed clearly beneath her eyes, and he could see a crease on her cheek from the fold of his pant leg. He remembered her in the car—the sweet weight of her head on his thighs and the feel of her silky hair beneath his palm.

Panic relaxed its grip and his heart jumped free. On impulse, he swooped down and caught her in his arms.

Her eyes widened. "Oh!" she said, looking at him as she might a kidnapper.

He should probably respond to her startled exclamation. Explain it wasn't an abduction, but a tradition. But the action and the explanation were so out of character that he felt a little startled himself.

Maybe he should forget the whole idea and set her down. Undecided, he pulled a breath into his lungs. Her perfume entered his system, speeding through it like coffee at 5:00 a.m. *What the hell*, he thought, ignoring a second, weaker squeeze of panic. *Some traditions are worth keeping.*

He stepped across the threshold.

Two more strides led him straight to another delicate, and, he suddenly realized with an inward groan, undiscussed issue.

"Now what?" she said as he halted, a little smile playing around her mouth.

"Exactly," he muttered. Now what? Did he take her to the bedroom? Put her down right here? Why hadn't they discussed the parameters of their marriage? Did she expect them to share a room, a bed? A tremor shook his muscles.

She frowned. "You'd better let me go. I weigh a ton."

"You've gotta be kidding. You're a feather." But he gently set her on her feet.

"Tell me that in a couple more months, when two babies are vying for room in here." She patted her still-flat tummy.

Relief bubbled. Babies. Tummy. Thank God he'd

put two and two together before he did something embarrassing, like coming on to Katie.

Pregnant. Of course Katie didn't expect any, uh, "attention" from her husband. Not only was she tired, but she was pregnant.

He turned toward the open door. "I'll just bring in my stuff."

The bags felt good in his hands. Maybe not as sweet as Katie, but definitely more familiar. He swung back around and saw a strange expression on her face. Worry. Nervousness. A tension that made her lick her lips. He watched her mouth darken with the added wetness.

Another tremor shook his muscles. *Stop looking at her lips,* he commanded himself. *You'll scare her even more.*

"Where's my room?" he asked, his voice booming into the quiet tension. "Put me someplace where I won't disturb your rest."

There. That should make it clear. She would know now that although he'd moved into her life, he hadn't also moved into her bed.

Saturday went about as awkwardly as the first day with a strange bridegroom could go, Katie thought. Though relieved to have ducked an intimate wedding night, the question of how they meant to go on lingered in her mind.

After meeting at the breakfast table—he was finishing his coffee and a bowl of cereal just as she arrived in the kitchen—they crossed paths only two more times that day. Once, when he emerged from the guest room and his briefcase long enough to ask about a pencil sharpener, and next, when he came into the kitchen and caught her as she tripped over the cord that connected her laptop on the nook table to the inconveniently-placed corner wall-socket.

With his hands gripping her upper arms and his green eyes so very close, she'd found it hard to catch her breath.

"You okay?" he asked.

A relative term. With her life completely changed, could she ever be okay? She took a step back, but his hands lingered on her.

"I'm fine." The whispery hoarseness in her voice embarrassed her. She cleared her throat. "How about you? Finding everything you need?"

"You have any extra administrative smarts hanging around?" He half smiled. "I'm going through Ryan's files and his end of the business takes some getting used to."

He still held her upper arms. The warmth of his hands bound her like his ring bound her finger...like this marriage bound the two of them.

"Did we do the right thing?" she asked him, suddenly needing to hear his reassurance.

Releasing her, he stepped back himself. "Just takes some getting used to," he said again, with a single curt nod, and was gone.

By Sunday morning, after examining and dissecting "just takes some getting used to" a dozen times, she decided he was exactly right. If they were going to have an acceptable kind of living arrangement, they had to get comfortable with each other. She climbed out of bed, determined to spend time with him to dispel the nervous jitters she felt in his presence.

Or maybe not. Because when she opened her bedroom door, she discovered he was gone.

No sign of him through the open door of the guest bedroom, any of the bathrooms, the front yard, back yard or garage. His car was gone, too.

Katie tried swallowing, but panic stuck like a lump in her throat. "He'll be back," she forced herself to say, surprised by how much she wanted it to be so.

And he did return. Within the hour, he entered the kitchen carrying a couple of plastic bags and a paper coffee cup from the local coffee bar.

She looked up casually from the newspaper she'd pretended to read the minute she heard the door open. Opening her mouth to greet him, "I thought you'd gone" blurted out instead. *Groan.*

His eyebrows rose. "Gone? You mean gone, gone?"

She shrugged.

The legs of the chair beside her scraped against the floor, but she refocused her gaze on the newspaper.

"I just went out for a few things," he said. "And some coffee. Yesterday I noticed the smell of it brewing bothered you."

Katie felt herself blush. So he'd been aware of her brief bout of nausea.

His hand came over hers. "I won't just take off on you, Katie. If I go, it'll only be because you ask me to."

At his touch, the customary jitters that always started their dance at the sight of him executed an intricate dip-and-whirl.

Katie pasted a smile on her face and quickly pulled out her captured hand to gaily pat the top of his. *Get comfortable with him.* "Thanks," she said with forced cheerfulness and made herself meet his gaze.

When she looked into his green eyes, solemn with his promise, her nerves became whirling dervishes. She shivered, but tried hiding it by widening her oh-so-casual and comfortable smile. "I thought we could do something together today." A walk? Out to lunch? Some kind of opportunity for face-to-face quiet conversation.

"Sure." He began rummaging in his plastic bags. "You can help me make a few repairs around here."

Repairs? She couldn't exactly complain as he pulled out several items: a new washer for the dripping kitchen faucet, a three-way light bulb for the one burned out in the corner living-room lamp, an electrical switch/plug combination so she could plug her laptop into a more convenient—and safer—outlet. But holding wrenches and passing the screwdriver didn't seem a good way to get comfortable with him.

After an hour, the only conversation they'd had

was his good-natured grumblings about her lousy set of tools, spiced with a few muttered oaths as he installed the new plug.

And after an hour of watching his capable hands and breathing in his spicy, masculine scent, her jitters had yet to calm.

And after that, they exchanged polite thank-yous and he excused himself by saying he was hitting the briefcase again.

Monday, Katie found Seth up earlier than on Saturday or Sunday, garbed in a dress shirt and khakis instead of a T-shirt and jeans. Nose to the newspaper, he seemed the same as the days before—polite but distant.

The thrill-and-chill fall of her heart upon seeing him was the same, too.

She pushed up the sleeves of her sweatshirt. "Good morning."

His eyes flicked her way and flicked back to the business pages of the newspaper. The sound he made was either a grunt or a "Hi."

So much for marriage.

Granted, they didn't know each other well, but she wanted a partnership, not a cohabitation.

He shifted in his chair, bunching muscles in his back, and the I-want-more thought tangled up with an I-want-him hormone surge. She ruthlessly sorted out the two, shoving away the hormones.

She had to remember their arrangement didn't need

passion. If his disinterest on their wedding night was any indication, he felt the same way.

She moved away, toward the gas range. But disinterest didn't explain his breathless response to the kiss they'd shared the night of his proposal. There had been other signs, too. Why, right now, if she quickly glanced his way—

She turned. *Yep,* she thought, she'd caught him looking at her. And she was fairly certain she didn't have a Stare Here sign pinned to the back of her jeans.

She sighed, her nerves humming along in merry excitement. Comfortable! She had to find a way to coexist with this man in a calm state. They needed to spend some quiet time together.

She thought fast. He was a man, and she was a cook. This should be easy. "What's your favorite thing to eat?"

The newspaper lowered, only revealing his eyes. His eyebrows lifted. "Favorite?" He paused, then his gaze shifted toward the empty bowl at his right. "Cornflakes, I guess, with a little dash of Fruit Loops on top."

She grimaced. "Not for breakfast." If she made his favorite meal tonight, his first workday night of marriage, they could spend a quiet evening becoming…friends.

His frown showed as a crease between his eyes. "Not for breakfast… Well, when I'm on a long trip I get cravings for beer nuts. And I always stick a couple of cans of those Vienna sausages in my bag in case I have to skip a meal."

"Beer nuts? *Vienna sausage?*" The thought of those, singly or in combination, threatened to bring on an attack of morning sickness. Katie inhaled a deep breath. She would think of an entrée later. "What about your favorite dessert?"

To her satisfaction, he lowered the paper to show a reminiscent smile tugging up the corners of his mouth. "That's easy. Mince pie. I love mince pie."

Katie gaped. "You've got to be kidding." Of all the things to be his favorite. "Mince isn't a food. It's...stuff." As a professional cook, she tried to remain open about other people's likes and dislikes. But mince!

"What kind of stuff?"

"Apples and cherries and ox hearts." She said the last ingredient with disgust.

"Oh." Seth's smile disappeared. "I see what you mean." The paper rose back up.

Darn, she'd lost him. She moved to the counter, jammed a piece of bread in the toaster, then tried again. "I was thinking about dinner tonight. Anything in particular sound good to you?"

The newspaper didn't move. He didn't say anything.

She walked around the table and knocked lightly on the newsprint wall separating them. After a moment, the paper lowered. "Anything in particular sound good?" she asked again. "For dinner?"

He shook his head, the shaggy ends of his hair brushing his wide shoulders, distracting her. "I think that mince recipe has squelched my appetite."

She groaned inwardly and turned away. The toaster popped, and she busied herself spreading strawberry jam. *No biggie. I'll just come up with something myself.* Maybe Izzy would have a good idea. Katie bit into the toast.

"I don't think I'll make it home for dinner tonight, anyway," Seth said.

She swung around. "What do you mean?"

The newspaper lay flat on the table now, and Seth scooted his chair to face her. "I'm sure I'll be working late." His gaze fixed on her mouth. "Very late."

"Oh." The warmth of his eyes on her momentarily diffused her disappointment.

Seth rose from his chair and walked to her. "Very, very late." His gaze stayed focused on her mouth.

Maybe he was going to kiss her. Heat rushed from her heart toward her face and her tongue crept out, moistening her lower lip.

"You got it," he said.

She thought a bit of regret touched his voice. "Got what?"

"Some jam." He reached out. "Just…there." One long, blunt finger touched the corner of her mouth, and then it was gone, and so was he.

And so was another opportunity to become comfortable in her marriage.

* * *

"So put one of those Hungry-Man fried-chicken things in the freezer and be done with it," Izzy suggested. "Let him figure out how to use the microwave. He's a big boy."

Katie sighed and riffled through the Katie's Candies paperwork on her kitchen table. Mondays were for ordering supplies and accounting, and her troubles with Seth and Izzy's solutions weren't making it any more pleasant.

"This isn't about food anyway," Izzy continued. She waggled a knowing finger Katie's way. "It's about sex."

Katie shook her head. "I told you. I just want to get to know him better. This is a two-bedroom marriage."

Izzy snorted. "Pu-leez. I've seen the way he looks at you."

Katie put her elbow on the table and rested her chin in her hand. "I just want more intimacy. We don't have to be...*intimate*. Just a frien—"

"Don't you dare say friendship." Izzy's orange curls shuddered in disgust. "What you—" The phone rang, stopping her tirade. Izzy grabbed the receiver, listened, then handed it toward Katie. "It's your *friend*," she said, rolling her eyes.

"How are you?" Seth's deep voice brushed softly down Katie's spine.

"I'm fine," she said, her hand involuntarily smoothing her hair. "Anything wrong?"

"Just checking on you." She could hear the click

of computer keys and imagined him paging through a spreadsheet while he spoke to her.

"You don't need to bother. Izzy's here."

He didn't respond to that. "No morning sickness? I noticed it seems to hit you about ten o'clock."

His concern sent a rush of warmth through her. "I seem okay today—thanks for asking." The brief struggles she'd had with nausea over the weekend hadn't recurred. "Izzy brought me some raspberry tea. Smells yucky, but I've been sipping it all morning."

"Raspberry tea." He repeated it as if he was committing the words to memory.

"How's your day going?"

"Fine." He suddenly sounded distracted, and she heard the indistinct murmur of another voice in the background. "I've got to go. Take care of my nieces or nephews."

"I will." Disappointment slowed her silly, quickening pulse. He'd been thinking about the *babies*, not her. A small sigh escaped.

A palpable hesitation came from the other side of the line. Seth cleared his throat. "I'll try to make it home for dinner tonight after all, Katie." He cleared his throat again.

"Maybe we can talk," she said, pleased.

"I'd like that."

Maybe we can talk.

Katie had held on to that thought all morning,

speeding through her paperwork and throwing out dinner ideas for Izzy's approval.

"You should have told him to bring home Chinese," the other woman had advised, but Katie wanted tonight's dinner to be something special.

She decided on vegetarian lasagna, and the sauce had simmered all afternoon. Chocolate sundaes for dessert, the vanilla-bean ice cream homemade and the topping an extra-special concoction of dark chocolate and Amaretto that Katie's Candies sold by the pint.

Maybe we can talk.

By 7:00 p.m., the entire meal was ready, and the only thing left to think about was what she would say.

She sat at the casually set dining-room table and played with the fringe on the ice-blue napkins. Best to be up front and ask about his expectations for the marriage. Tell him that to cement the family they would make with the children, she wanted an emotional partnership. She nodded briskly, approving her own commonsense, well-chosen words.

She'd turned the oven down twice before she finally heard Seth's key turn in the lock. His slow tread on the hardwood hallway sounded tired, and when he glanced into the dining room she saw that his tie was unknotted and hung limply over his chest like the tongues of a pair of exhausted dogs.

He met her gaze, groaned, and dropped his briefcase with a *clunk.* "You went to a lot of trouble." His hand rumpled his hair. "I can smell it and I can see it. Damn. I'm sorry I'm so late. You shouldn't have waited for me.''

Katie's stomach jitter-bugged downward. Even tired, he looked good. ''We agreed to talk.'' She pushed her chair away from the table. ''Can I get you something to drink before we eat?''

He propped one shoulder against the doorjamb and wearily closed his eyes. ''I'm too tired to do both. I think I'll just eat.''

Worry twisted Katie's overactive stomach. A tired man wasn't a talking man. ''Can't I get you some milk? A beer?''

Although his eyes opened, he shook his head.

Another worry-twist. ''How about a V8?'' she said, gesturing toward the glass in front of her. ''That's what I'm drinking. It's supposed to boost your energy.'' She jumped up from her chair and tucked a swinging strand of hair behind her ear.

Seth's gaze lazily followed the movement and he smiled tiredly. ''Must make your hair shiny, too.''

Her laugh even sounded nervous to herself, but she played along. ''Oh, yes,'' she said. ''And keeps your teeth white and your skin clear.''

His smile gained a sly kick at one corner. ''I think, Beauty, the old wives credit something else for *that*.''

Without responding, Katie beat a cowardly retreat toward the kitchen. *Whew.* Obviously, she needed a little sustenance herself before she could handle Seth and sexy innuendo.

As a precautionary measure, both plates held hefty

portions of lasagna, salad and bread when she returned to the table. Seth accepted his gratefully, with a promise to later clear the dishes and wash all the pots and pans.

Katie tried reminding him of their purpose. "Maybe we can do them together after we talk."

But with each bite, Seth seemed to retreat further from her. He didn't even look at her, his attention focused solely on his plate and his fork.

Katie ate a small portion of lasagna, then played with the magenta curls of radicchio in her salad, the feeling she was being ignored growing steadily. Hadn't he agreed to talk? she grumbled to herself. "I'm beginning to wish I was covered in tomato sauce and ricotta."

Clank. His fork clattered to his plate and his startled gaze jumped to her face. "What?"

She smiled sweetly. "Bad day?"

"Hellish." He gathered up his fork, bent his head and tried going for his food again.

"Maybe a little Parmesan instead of face powder."

His head stayed low but his eyes swiveled her way. "*What* are you talking about?"

"I'm talking about talking. You. Me. You agreed to. I want to. But unless I transform into pasta and tomato sauce, I don't think I'm going to get your attention."

He laid the fork down quietly this time. "I'm sorry, Katie. I have...too much on my mind. What did you want to talk about?"

"I...uh..."

Great. Now that she had his attention, she was too wimpy to jump right into discussing their marriage. She squeezed her fork. "Why don't you start by telling me what's bugging you?"

He gave her a funny look and choked out a laugh. "I don't know...."

She frowned. "I assume it's Ends of the Earth. Did something go wrong at the office?"

He grimaced. "The business is some of it. It's four weeks and counting to the board of directors meeting. We need a workable reorganization plan by then, or..."

"Or?"

He made a throat-cutting gesture and a c-crrr-tch sound between his teeth.

Chills washed down her arms. If Ends of the Earth went under, what would keep Seth in the area? What would happen to their marriage? "You don't think... You're not going to lose the company?"

He shrugged. "Probably not. But unless I get real good at Ryan's responsibilities real soon, we may be in trouble."

"I didn't know."

His mouth turned down. "There's a reason Ryan and I worked the company the way we did. I'm lousy at the desk stuff, and he is—wasn't." His frown deepened. "But I have to keep the company going. Ryan would want that for his children."

Katie reached across the table and touched the back of his hand. "You can do it, Seth. I know you can."

His palm turned upward and his long, strong fingers closed over hers. Heat seeped from her fingernails toward her wrist, where the pulse pounded faster. *Thup-thup-thup-thup-thup.*

She licked her lips.

He looked away, but didn't let go of her hand. "What did you want to talk about?"

"Me?" Her voice squeaked, as if his hand held her vocal chords instead of her fingers. She felt his touch everywhere. "I...uh..." Her gaze found his and she couldn't form another word. Heat prickled her cheeks and she decided that green was her favorite eye color in all the world.

He suddenly let go of her hand. "Can it wait until another time?" Without even pausing for her answer, he gathered up their plates and headed toward the kitchen. "I can't do this. I've got to get to work."

He swung around and looked at her, a plate in each hand, still retreating in the direction of the kitchen sink. "Distracting...crazy... How'm I gonna make it? How many months...? Oh, God," he muttered to himself before he spun again and slid the plates on the kitchen counter.

Katie clasped her hands, covering the warmth his fingers had left behind. "Are you okay?"

Nodding vigorously, he kept his back to her and pulled down the dishwasher door. "I'm fine when I concentrate on work. I've got to pull an all-nighter. I haven't been sleeping anyway.''

Puzzled, Katie got up from the table. "I'll help—"

"No!" His shoulders tensed. "Go to bed. You're pregnant. *Pregnant.* Pregnant women need sleep." It sounded like he was talking to himself.

It also sounded like tonight was not the night to talk about their marriage.

Still rubbing her Seth-warmed hand, Katie moved slowly down the hallway toward her bedroom.

The moment Seth heard the telltale click of Katie's bedroom door, he dashed to the portable phone in the kitchen and stared at the speed-dial list on its spine. He stabbed at the pound sign and the one and collapsed in a chair in the breakfast nook when Dan answered the phone.

"Just talk to me. The 49ers. Even your all-time hero, Joe Montana. Anything.''

"Is that you, Seth? What's the problem, buddy?'' Dan sounded jovial, but surprised.

"Just talk. I need distraction.''

"Distraction? Well, let's talk about your honeymoon weekend, then. I was going to leave you alone another couple of days, but what the hay, since you called me—"

Seth groaned. "Did anyone ever tell you you're a cruel man? *Not* honeymoons, please." The last thing he wanted to discuss was what he hadn't done with Katie. The woman was making him nuts. Her hair, her fragrance, the way she'd looked at him when he'd come home that night.

"Cruel? I helped Izzy pick out that black lace number for Katie. I told her, a man likes black."

Seth wasn't listening. He was still thinking of the two unending weekend days he'd spent avoiding Katie, pretending to work when all the time he'd been turned on by the swing of her gilt hair against her shoulder blades, the faint outline of her breasts against her shirts, the sweet tingle her smile started in his belly.

"You do like black, don't you?"

Seth tuned in to his friend. "What are you talking about? Black what?"

"Nightgowns, underwear, whatever." Dan cleared his throat. "I don't want you to think I got too cozy with your wife's stuff. Izzy just asked my opinion on teddies. Black, white, or red."

"Izzy bought Katie a black teddy?" Seth refused to allow a picture of Katie wearing one form in his mind.

Damn, he had lousy self-control.

Dan's voice burst the glorious daydream. "That was what was in the box she gave to Katie on your wedding night. Remember, at our house? Did you like it?"

Seth squeezed the bridge of his nose. "What the hell are you talking about? I didn't see her nightgown. Katie's pregnant." And he needed to remember that.

A long silence buzzed across the line. A confusing silence.

"Dan?"

"Uh, Seth, ol' buddy..." An unidentifiable note had entered Dan's voice. "Just a minute, I'm moving to the garage." More silence and some weird shuffling noises. Then Dan spoke again. "I wanted to get out of Izzy's hearing. We're alone now, Seth."

"How...special."

Dan ignored the sarcasm. "Uh, buddy, how much do you know about pregnant women?"

Seth trotted out his entire volume of facts. "Nine months. Raspberry tea for nausea. Braxton Hicks are pretend contractions."

A gusty laugh wheezed over the phone. "That's it?"

Seth searched his memory. "Pretty much."

"Do you realize that pregnant women can have sex?"

An I've-been-had feeling thumped Seth in the solar plexus. "Say what?"

"Pregnant women can have sex. Pretty much up until the end." He chuckled. "They even want it—sometimes."

"You're not saying... You don't mean..." Sweat popped out on Seth's forehead. "Women pregnant with twins?"

"I don't think Izzy would buy Katie a negligee if Katie's doctor had been concerned."

Seth opened his mouth. Closed it. Opened it again,

then wiped the dampness off his brow. "Dammit, Dan!"

Dan's chuckles threatened to turn into guffaws. "You really didn't know? Didn't Katie mention—" Guffawing took over.

Seth let the sounds of hilarity wash over him. Why hadn't Katie mentioned it? What must she be thinking? He pictured her at the dining-room table that night, candlelight dancing across her hair, in her eyes, making her so attractive he'd nearly grabbed her up right then and there.

"Hell, Cooper," he muttered to himself. "You coulda had a V8."

5

Seth rinsed the lasagna pan and set it on the counter to dry. Cocking his head, he listened for sounds of Katie moving about the house. No, she was still in her room, just like she'd been since they'd finished eating.

He should talk to her. With determined steps, he left the kitchen and walked quietly down the hall. He needed to tell her he was dumbfounded, or better yet, just plain dumb to realize that pregnancy didn't preclude sex.

He would just have to admit how little he knew about the entire baby-growing process. Once the, uh, seed had been planted, so to speak, he just thought that was a row a man no longer should, uh, hoe.

Groaning silently, he halted outside Katie's bedroom door. He was not so dumb that he would repeat that little metaphor to her. And could he really say he hadn't known? Or was it that in some dark corner inside he had not wanted to get close to her? Ready to knock, he lifted his hand, then quickly stuffed it into his pocket. For that matter, why hadn't Katie brought up the issue herself?

Easy. She probably felt as awkward about the situation as he did right now.

Or else she was happy with the situation just as it was.

He raised his hand again to knock, staring at the slice of meager light showing beneath the door. What was he going to say? "Excuse me, but did you want a partner in bed?"

A black-teddied-Katie image leaped into his mind, but Seth shoved his hand in his pocket again. So the idea made his groin ache and his imagination run wild. Wasn't it safer to keep things as they were?

The more he thought about it, although he would always want to be a father to Ryan's kids, he wasn't sure what he or Katie wanted from this marriage. Things would go more smoothly the less involved they remained.

Sex made things messy. Heck, just the idea of it had played havoc with his concentration for the past few days. And women, he reflected—at the risk of some angry feminist reading his thoughts and contracting an assassin—women got so *emotional* about sex.

Everybody knew Seth was lousy at emotions, just like his father. When feelings became too intense, Seth always wandered off.

And true to form, he noted ironically, *I'm doing it again.* His gaze took in the dining room. Without realizing what he'd done, he'd walked away from Katie's door and returned to the relative safety of his briefcase and business.

Yeah, he had a better chance of sticking by Katie if he stayed out of her bed. With determination, he flipped open the brass locks on the leather satchel.

Katie stared at the digital readout on the scale in the tiny cubby she called her workout room. *No more lasagna leftovers.*

How could she have gained so much weight in so short a time? Only a week had passed since she'd made that lasagna and actually, Seth had polished off the leftovers days ago.

The scale had never been this high—and even after a thirty-minute session on the treadmill!

She stepped off the rubber tread and stepped back on, peering again at the quickly climbing numbers, for the first time glad there continued to be so much distance between herself and Seth. A wife who doubled in size overnight could be disconcerting!

She ran a hand over her abdomen. No doubt about it, the extra weight was right *there*. Even the black color of her unitard couldn't disguise the burgeoning pot of her belly.

Tears stung the corners of her eyes. Of course, she should be happy that the twins were growing, but suddenly everything seemed so—

"Katie." Air wooshed through the room as the door to the hallway swung open.

"Seth!" Katie kept her back to the door. After waking early, she'd crept past his closed door to the exercise room, hoping to finish before he awakened.

"You okay?" Concern had entered his voice.

She stayed on the scale, still loath to face him. At this moment all she wanted was to be left alone. "Fine."

Darn it, she sounded choked up. She swallowed. "What is it you need?"

"You're sure you're okay?" His voice came closer.

She didn't have a towel or T-shirt—not a thing to cover up a body that was beginning to feel like it was growing by the second. She edged one sneakered foot over the scale's readout and looked casually over her shoulder. "Fine, I said. What do you need?"

One thing he needed, she realized, was a haircut. The shaggy locks, rumpled and damp from the shower, hung almost to his shoulders. Bare shoulders.

Katie gulped. No fair. To catch her first glimpse of bare-to-the-waist Seth when she was feeling blue about her own body. That sting of tears pricked her eyes again and she looked away from his wide chest and hard abs. *No fair.*

"Katie—"

"Maybe we could talk later, Seth." *When I have a circus tent covering me.* "Better yet, call me when you get to the office." Her voice had that silly hitch in it again.

She tried to make her belly seem smaller by

straightening her shoulders. It didn't work. Again she was very glad her relationship with Seth had stayed impersonal. *Nonphysical.*

But then he gripped her arm and spun her gently around. "What's the matter?" A crease appeared between his green eyes.

She had to take a step toward his bare chest because she had to get off the scale. No man should see those numbers.

Her feet shuffled off the tread and she kept her gaze on his chin. It was kind of scruffy, like he'd missed a few spots shaving. *Makes me feel a little better.*

"What did you need?" she asked again, casually crossing her arms over her waistline.

"I was looking for bandages."

Suddenly she noticed that a washcloth wrapped one of his hands.

"My God, what happened?" She grabbed his wrist and pulled away the cloth. Blood seeped from a shallow cut across his palm.

"A minor run-in with a new razor blade. Bandages?"

She pressed the cloth back on the wound and tugged him down the hall to her bathroom. She could have just handed him the bandage box and the antiseptic, but instead she pushed him down on the toilet seat and cleansed and bandaged his hand herself.

Maybe because she liked the smell of his shampoo.

With the last plastic strip fastened, she caught a glimpse of her reflection in the bathroom mirror.

Messy hair, the unitard, *the stomach*. Behind her, the hard muscles of Seth's body. *No fair*. She went for the casual arm-cross again and started out of the bathroom.

He caught hold of her. "Something *is* wrong."

His fingers on her forearm felt hot and firm and she reminded herself she liked things between them to stay impersonal. "Nothing's wrong. Don't you have to get to work?"

"Maybe I've been spending too much time at the office. Something's wrong."

Without warning, tears filled her eyes. *How embarrassing*. This was not the time to succumb to weepiness. Not until he was gone for another megaday at Ends of the Earth. Her face averted from him, she blinked rapidly. "I'd rather we stay...businesslike. It's silly, anyway."

His fingers didn't release her arm. His bandaged hand grasped her chin and turned her face his way. His eyes appeared primeval green. "Tell me."

"God, I feel so stupid." She jerked her chin from his hand. "It's my—my body, okay? I'm starting to look pregnant and I feel..."

To give him credit, he didn't let go of her, although his face wore one of those strictly male, I-could-be-in-big-trouble-here expressions. A tinge of red darkened his cheekbones. "You feel?"

She sighed. "Kind of...ugly, okay? Undesirable."

Seth stood so fast his movements blurred. One moment he faced her, sitting down, the next he was behind her, standing, pulling her back against the heated hardness of his chest.

"Undesirable?" his voice said almost harshly. With his chin against her temple, he directed her gaze toward their reflection in the mirror.

"I see beauty," he said in her ear. "Generosity, warmth, fortitude." One hand left her shoulder and smoothed down her arm to her wrist. He took her fingers and curved them over her belly.

His heart beat strongly, slowly, against her back. "I see a woman growing joy in her body."

It was exactly the right thing to say. Katie savored his words, savored his warmth, but, afraid to break the moment of closeness, said nothing.

After a few more heartbeats, he patted her shoulder and moved away. In the doorway, he paused. "And undesirable?" A strange, almost-pained expression crossed his face. "For the record, Katie, pregnant or not, I think you're sexy as hell."

Her heart plunged toward her growing stomach. "No fair," she whispered to his retreating back. "No fair."

Seth's running shoes pounded satisfyingly hard against the pavement. Although it was noontime, the sun didn't penetrate the famous thickness of the San Francisco fog.

He drew in a lungful of moist, cold air. "Damn, it's good to be running again."

Dan lumbered beside him. "I left my computer for

this?'' He wheezed. ''Even after a week, I'm so sore Izzy has to Ben-Gay me every night.''

Seth groaned. ''Don't bring up the benefits of marital bliss.''

Dan grinned while sucking in air through his teeth. ''Not my fault you don't have bridal bennies.''

''Can't we talk about something else? I won't go so far as the 'Niners, but you can talk Raiders football to me. What's happening in Oakland these days?''

They reached a red traffic light and Dan stopped with obvious relief. ''Don't tell me you're going to run in place,'' he said, holding on to the light post for support.

''Gotta do something to get this energy out of my system.''

''Aha! The truth finally comes out. This isn't an urge to get *in* shape, but an urge to get someone else's shape out of your mind.''

Seth smiled, picturing Katie as he'd seen her this morning. Slender, in black workout gear and worried over the pregnancy changes to her body. God, who would have thought that a rounding belly could turn him on as much as her blue eyes?

But more than that, her inner self, as true-blue as her eyes, was getting to him, too. Every day he thought of the generous support she'd given Ryan and Karen, her instantaneous decision to go from aunt to mommy, of the faith she'd exhibited in his ability to keep the company together.

''I see that smile,'' Dan accused.

The light changed and Seth shut up his friend by dragging him through the crosswalk.

Dan persisted. "You won't get off that easy. The woman's creeping under your skin."

Seth saw no reason to lie. "Living with her is making me nuts," he admitted. "Frustrated. Crazy. Unable to focus. I have to work past midnight every evening because I'm at about one-quarter concentration."

"Well, then, forget this business-only marriage—" Dan's voice rose "—and take your wife to bed!"

A pair of thirty-something women in business suits, athletic socks and walking shoes glared at them.

Seth choked back a laugh. "Shh. You'll get us arrested."

Dan wiped at the sweat rolling down his face. "Look down at those swoops on your running shoes and take a clue. 'Just do it!'"

Seth laughed again. The hell of it was, the idea of forgetting his resolve and taking Katie to bed grew more appealing every day. Make that every hour. "Have you smelled that woman's perfume?" He was beginning to discover it everywhere. Wisps of it escaped his briefcase in the morning. Teased him from his pillowcase at night.

"You need—to make this—a real marriage," Dan said between gasps.

Seth looked at his friend closely. "Do you know something I should know? Katie's actually... interested?" Ever since that one kiss, he'd

wondered if any of the reactions he would normally
attribute to arousal were what she'd claimed then—
whacked-out hormones.

Dan shook his head. "Izzy spills nothin'." He
sucked in air. "But I think you owe it to your company."

"What?"

"Yeah. A little nooky and you'll be one hundred
percent again."

Dan grunted with obvious appreciation as Seth
slowed the pace a bit. "I don't know, Dan...."

"For God's sake, you're a married man. For better
or worse." He wheezed in some air. "And nothing's
worse than unrequited lust."

Seth could only agree with that.

Dan pressed his point. "Once you, uh, *normalize*
things with Katie, your work problems will clear up,
too."

The logic was a little fuzzy. "But how do we know
Katie's interested?"

"Talk about it. Find out."

Seth sent a glance to red-faced Dan. "Easy for you
to say. And didn't you tell me pregnant women can
be a little...quirky?"

Dan grunted in agreement. "There is that. Growin'
babies is hell on a man, you know."

"Jeez, Dan, and I'm sure it's a walk in a garden
for a woman."

"Pregnant females are touchy, okay?" Dan defended between wheezes. "Raring to go. Sleepy,

sleepless. Happy. Sad." He shrugged. "But when all systems are go—" more wheezes "—watch out."

Dan's blissful grin decided Seth. He wanted a smile like that. He wanted that kind of memory. "So, I should go to bed with my wife."

Dan grunted affirmatively.

The idea sounded more sensible by the mile. "I owe it to the company," Seth tried out.

Dan slanted him sly glance. "Unless you're doing it for your heart."

Seth speeded up. "I've got our five-mile runs for that."

Katie's personal line rang midafternoon. She'd left her detached candy kitchen to retrieve a cookbook she had in the house. The phone rang again, and she tucked the cookbook under her arm, then grabbed up the receiver.

"How are you this afternoon?"

Katie shivered. Although she'd come to expect Seth's daily phone calls, his voice still did funny things to her skin. "I'm fine. Busy. Izzy and I are trying out something new."

"I'm licking my lips. The staff loved the truffles you had me bring in this morning, by the way."

She tried not to think of Seth's lips—and thinking of licking them was out of the question altogether. "What about Grace? I thought she might like the mocha."

"Best yet, she said." He paused. "But that's not why I called." A second long pause.

Another of those shivers rolled over Katie's skin. Seth's calls were usually just brief check-ins. Normally, they would already be exchanging goodbyes.

More silence thinned her nerves. "Well, uh, why did you call?"

"Be—"

Katie's business line rang. "Darn, I have to get that. Izzy's up to her eyeballs in chocolate leaves," she told Seth. Clutching the portable receiver, she hurried over to the business phone in the kitchen.

June Carver, the hospitality chairperson for the local Junior League chapter, had discovered an immediate need for chocolates for luncheon-party favors. Katie jotted down the order, then swiftly hung up.

"You still there?" she asked Seth.

"Breathing." He didn't say any more.

Katie, her sense of something different about this call even stronger now, didn't know what to do. "Well, uh, so how's business going?"

"Better. Maybe. That's why I'm calling."

Finally. But she frowned. "Calling about Ends of the Earth? I don't imagine I can help unless you need to know something about chocolate."

"Nothing like that." Silence again followed.

Katie swallowed and found herself filling the quiet. "Ryan would be glad you're working so hard," she said. She had to say *something.* "He loved the catalog company."

"We both did. I still do." A smidgen of ease entered his voice. "We liked working together, even though we were so different."

Katie smiled, thinking of her brother-in-law. "Family was terribly important to Ryan."

"To me, too, in my own way," he said quietly.

"I didn't mean—"

"I know, but for years Ryan and I were the only support each other had. I don't want to let go of what we built together. I want to pass it on to...Ryan's children."

Ryan's children. He didn't think of the babies as his, or theirs. She swallowed her disappointment. "You said you needed my help?"

The silence was shorter this time. Then his voice blurted over the line. "I, uh, don't know too much about pregnancy."

Katie pulled a glass from the cupboard and filled it with water. "I probably know a little more, but what does that have to do with the business? I don't imagine the catalog targets the pregnant segment of the population."

"I didn't know that pregnant women can have sex."

She slammed the glass to the countertop, splashing water over her wrist. Stunned into silence, she merely listened.

"Ignorant as it sounds, I just assumed we couldn't have a physical side to our marriage because you were pregnant."

"Oh." Relief sluiced through Katie. His assumption explained a lot, but didn't quiet a bubble of anxiety that rose in the pit of her stomach. What did he want to do now?

"So, now that I know better," he said, "I wondered—" He hesitated momentarily. "I wondered if maybe we could talk about it tonight. Our, uh, physical relationship."

Katie's fingers tightened on the pencil she'd used to take down June's order. "Sure," she said, her voice not sounding half as dry as her throat suddenly was. "That would be fine."

He clicked off, as if he couldn't do it fast enough, and she stared down at her notes. This afternoon she had to help Izzy finish the chocolate leaves. Call in another order for the chocolate she used as the base for her candies. Track down yellow boxes and violet ribbon to wrap the Junior League candies, as requested.

Decide whether or not she wanted to go to bed with her husband.

Seth checked his watch—8:00 p.m. "Damn." He'd thought to spend only an hour on the inventory report after the eight-to-fivers had rushed out of the office. But now it was three hours later, and Katie waited at home.

Katie.

He slammed shut his briefcase and grabbed his keys before the thought of her could paralyze him. Suggesting that they change the sleeping arrangements had made sense while running with Dan, had made sense while conducting the awkwardly tense phone call to her. Made perfect sense to the needs of his body.

But would it make sense to Katie?

He sped toward home in the Explorer, his mind running over and over the image of her in the bathroom that morning, gently bandaging his hand, then confessing the strangeness of being pregnant.

He groaned. Maybe now wasn't such a good time to suggest sleeping together. Maybe she would say no because she felt awkward about her body.

But he could change her feelings about herself. Damn right, he could. His hands would trace the round curves, absorb the warmth of her skin, impart the knowledge that he found her beautiful.

A shift on the seat didn't ease the tightening fit of his pants. *Calm down, Cooper,* he thought as he pulled into the driveway. *First she has to say yes.*

Despite the caution, he let himself into the house, his body still in a state of arousal and his heart slamming against his chest in anticipation. Seth ran his hands nervously through his hair. *Would she or wouldn't she?*

Delicious smells led him to the kitchen. A roasted chicken rested on a carving board. Two plates sat on the countertop, ready to be filled. A fire burned low in the brick fireplace.

At the breakfast-nook table, Katie's head was pillowed on her arms, her face turned toward him. With her eyelashes shadowing against her cheeks, her candlelight-yellow hair spilling over one shoulder to puddle on the scarred oak table, she slept.

Seth's heart shuddered to a halt and childhood memories rushed forward.

There had been nights and nights and nights exactly like this in his childhood. His mother cooking dinners for a man who was never on time to eat them. His mother, the dinner gone cold, sitting up and waiting for her husband to come home. His mother left behind by her husband, abandoned, and then abandoning Ryan and Seth for the well of unhappiness she hungered in for the rest of her life.

What if he hurt Katie the way his father had hurt his mother? God, he couldn't let that happen to her.

He stared at her for a moment longer. *Take her to bed, Cooper,* his conscience urged. *Take her to bed but don't join her there.*

With quiet footsteps he walked over to the table. Bending his knees, he gathered her limp and heavy-with-sleep body into his arms. She mumbled something, but still deep in dreamland, her body rested against his as he carried her down the hallway to her bedroom.

One light glowed by the bed. Her breath rushed softly against his neck as he bent his knees again to grab the comforter and pull it back. *Set her down and go.*

He ignored the unceasing rat-a-tat-tat of his pulse as his arms grazed the smooth coolness of the bedsheets. *Katie's bed.* His cheek slid against her smooth hair, and strands caught in his evening beard as he lowered her to the mattress.

He loosened her sneakers and slipped them off. She could sleep in her socks, leggings and tunic. No way was he getting any closer to skin.

Her eyes opened as he tucked the pale blue comforter beneath her chin. Puzzlement made a crease between her brows. "Seth," she said drowsily.

He took a breath. "Shh. Go to sleep, Katie." The bedroom door looked miles away.

And her hand gripped his wrist before he could make it there. "I fell asleep," she said. "Sorry."

"That's okay. You need your rest." *And I need to remember one of the first lessons I learned about life—love causes pain.* He didn't want to be the source of Katie's.

Although her eyes were still drowsy, her mouth turned down. "Are you going?"

"Yes." *Right now.* But his feet didn't move.

"Kiss me good-night."

Now that was a bad idea. His libido was in shock, having gone from a state of arousal to a state of strict control, and now, back to arousal again.

No use fooling himself about that.

Her fingers tightened on his wrist. They didn't have any real strength, of course, but they bound him inextricably.

"Just one," he said, to set the rules.

She tugged him down to her, and he followed willingly, ready to pull back after just the slightest touch, the slightest brush of her lips.

And then he met their warmth, their smooth softness. She opened, her warm breath rushing over his mouth.

The evident drowsiness in her eyes and the languor in her limbs forced him to chastely end the kiss. He brushed one more across her forehead, then stepped away.

As he suspected she might, she immediately closed her eyes and snuggled deep into the covers.

At the doorway, he hesitated, looking back at Katie. *God, she's beautiful.* His chest heaved in a gulp of air. Had he really convinced himself that doing the deed with her would take away this agonizing need?

With the taste of her kiss on his mouth and the effects still throbbing throughout his body, he knew that crawling into bed with her wouldn't change a thing. Climaxing inside the tight glove of her body wouldn't bring an end to her preoccupation of his thoughts...or to his desires.

Seth closed his eyes. And if in taking her to bed she came to care for him, he would hurt her when he wrenched away from those emotions. As his father had.

And if you care for her, you'll be hurt if she leaves you. The thought came unbidden, and was immediately dismissed. This wasn't about him.

The low glow of the lamp warmed the cool blond of her hair. "I never want to hurt you," he said softly, then flipped out the light.

6

Standing before the worktable in the candy kitchen, Izzy rubbed the small of her back. "Five weeks to go! It seems forever."

"Try five months," Katie said, although she smiled sympathetically. "Are you too excited to wait?"

"And nervous. Dan, too." Izzy put a second hand to her back. "Now that my due date is getting closer, he doesn't want me to spend any time alone."

Alone. The word echoed through Katie like a tolling bell, resonating unpleasantly against her heart. She knelt before a cardboard box and pulled out a stack of small, yellow, flattened cartons. If not for Seth, she would be pregnant alone, raising the babies alone. What did it matter that alone was how she spent her nights?

A memory from the week before, him carrying her to bed, his mouth soft on hers, created an ache between her legs. Her neck heated and she tried thinking of something else.

I never want to hurt you.

A week ago, his words had drifted through drowsiness into her consciousness. Since then, both had studiously avoided the bed-sharing issue. One thing she'd discovered they had in common was an ability to sidestep awkward subjects.

It's what you get for marrying a stranger.

Apparently he thought it better to keep their relationship platonic. If that was what he wanted, if they could only have an nonphysical partnership—a *par-ent*ship for the sake of the twins—then fine.

She remembered his green eyes burning down at her as he'd ended their kiss. But he did want her, she whispered inwardly; he did.

Not that it made her feel any better.

"What's the matter? More trouble with Seth?" Izzy still rubbed at her back, a look of concern overlying the discomfort on her face.

Katie straightened and put the carton stack on the worktable beside the spools of violet ribbon. "Why don't you go home, Iz? I can finish here."

Izzy frowned. "You have the entire Junior League order to wrap. It'll take hours."

"Go home, Iz." Katie needed to put Seth out of her head, and knowing Izzy, he would be a prime target of conversation over the candy wrapping.

Izzy's red eyebrows snapped together. "Something's wrong between you and your life-mate."

"*Roommate,*" Katie corrected. "It's more physically and emotionally accurate."

"That man—"

Katie interrupted Izzy's huff. "I'll crank up the

music, put my brain into neutral and my hands in high gear. I don't want to think right now, about Seth or anything else.''

Izzy protested some more, but Katie insisted she leave. Losing herself and her doubts in music and the monotonous actions of individually wrapping the large candy order sounded perfect.

As Izzy let herself out, Katie crossed to the boom box in one corner of the room and upped the volume of the Mary Chapin Carpenter CD from background to semi-blasting.

Brrring. Through the boogie piano beat Katie caught the ring of her personal phone-line. She noted the time—three o'clock. The call was probably Seth, checking in.

Biting her lip, she let it ring again. Roommates could let the machine pick up when roommates called. Another ring. A roommate could appreciate the concern behind the habitual midday how-are-you without subjecting herself to her roommate's deep and sexy voice.

That line abruptly stopped ringing, and the business line took over. With a groan, Katie crossed to pick it up. Although she guessed the caller, she couldn't ignore possible business.

''Katie, is everything all right?'' Seth's voice barely broke through the music bopping through the room.

''I'm fine. Fine and busy.'' The deep tones of his voice got lost in the melodic strains of the next song.

"I can hardly hear you. Can you turn the music down?"

Katie smiled grimly. "Can't hear you very well. I'll talk to you later. Thanks for the call!"

"Wait!"

She had hundreds of chocolates to wrap. Music to sing along to. Men, and her wayward desire for one in particular, to forget. "Eight?" She pretended to mishear him. "I'll see you then!"

"Hold it!"

She couldn't think of a rhyming hour fast enough.

"I need to talk to you." He got that out before she could even fake a logical misunderstanding.

Katie thought of the pot of herbal tea he made for her every morning. The newspaper turned to an article on infant rearing at her place at the kitchen table today. "Just a minute, let me turn the music down."

She didn't curb her resigned sigh. She still wanted out of this phone call ASAP.

Mary Chapin started whispering about kissing. Katie turned the music off altogether.

"Okay," she said into the quiet. "You said you needed to talk. Can you make it quick? I'm very busy today."

"You've been very busy for the entire last week," he grumbled. "I've hardly seen you."

Katie shrugged. "You leave pretty early in the morning."

"You go to bed pretty early at night."

To avoid you. "Is there something you need?"

He grumbled again. "I need to know how you are. How you're doing."

Katie picked up a fat stack of tissue-paper squares with the Katie's Candy logo and slapped it onto the worktable next to the cartons.

"The babies are fine," she said pleasantly.

"Good. I—"

"Gotta go now." The shorter the call, the more impersonal she could keep it.

"Don't hang up."

Something in Seth's voice made her hold on the phone tighten. "What is it? Is there a problem?"

"We, um…" His hesitation came over the line.

"We, um, what?" Katie could tell he was almost embarrassed.

"A present was delivered to us here today."

"A present?"

He cleared his throat. "Wrapped in white with a big silver ribbon. 'To Mr. and Mrs. Seth Cooper.'"

"Oh." Katie's face burned. Mr. and Mrs. Seth Cooper shouldn't sound so nice. "Who is it from?"

He defrogged his throat again. "Your mother and father."

"What?" Katie nearly fell into her chair in surprise. "How do you know? What is it?"

"An engraved silver pitcher."

"It can't be from my mother and father. They divorced ages ago." Painfully, in the longest, most drawn-out way possible.

"Yeah, you told me that before. But they obviously

got together on the gift. Even the card has a message from each of them.''

Knowing her parents, because ''Ends of the Earth'' came in the address book before ''McKay,'' they'd gone the convenience route and sent the gift to the catalog offices. ''Still,'' she mused, ''it's an amazing first.''

''They don't usually cooperate?''

Katie gritted her teeth. ''The only other thing I remember them getting together on was concocting ways to make Karen's and my life miserable.''

''Sounds a little harsh,'' Seth said warily.

The familiar pain rose from her heart toward her throat. ''They should have put us first and they never did,'' Katie defended her bitterness. She rubbed a hand over her face, remembering the ever-present tension. ''They always made us choose. Mom or Dad. Dad or Mom.''

Lost in memories, she hardly heard Seth's question. ''Split custody?''

''Just about fifty-fifty.'' Sunday night through Wednesday night with her father. The other half of the week at her mother's.

''Fair enough.''

A burst of old anger swallowed up her reticence. ''Yeah, if you wanted to spend Dad's days telling what we did with Mom. And Mom's part of the week being grilled about Dad's newest girlfriend.''

''Sounds...unpleasant.''

Katie felt the resentment rise. ''Unbalanced is more

like it. Dadless some days. Momless the others. But most of all, familyless.''

"Hell, Katie. I didn't mean to upset you."

The intimate sympathy in his voice reminded her of what she'd revealed. Roommates didn't share dirty laundry. Katie pushed away from the worktable, ready to hang up the phone. "Sorry to be so strident. Forget—''

"And that's what you want for the twins? A family?"

More than anything. "Karen became my family," she said quietly. "I don't want to do less for her children.''

"Ryan would want that, too." Seth spoke with certainty. "I'm committed to doing the best I can for the twins, Katie."

His words warming her, she squeezed the phone tighter. "Thank you, Seth. We need to appreciate the miracle.''

"Miracle?"

She wanted him to understand. "This isn't pregnant in the usual way. This isn't 'Oops,' or 'Wasn't that easy.''' Her free hand crept over her abdomen. "The twins are a product of Karen and Ryan's intense desire.''

"And love, Katie." His voice hoarsened. "Your love.''

Her heart swelled, pushing toward her throat. "Yours, too, Seth." But that sounded way too personal. Too much…not like a roommate. "For your brother, and for his children," she hurriedly added.

"Yeah," he said, his voice gruff.

"Yeah," she echoed, as he clicked off.

She replaced the receiver slowly. It was getting harder and harder to keep him in her life but out of her heart.

Seth drove home from the office that evening, his mind still on the afternoon phone call to Katie. Damn, but she brought out the most unexpected feelings in him. Empathy. Sympathy. Understanding. *Ties* that connected them more securely than their I'll-be-Daddy you-be-Mommy agreement.

But ties were exactly what he didn't want.

Katie got to him every time, though. A smile, a tear, a stroke of her silken skin drew him, then drove him to want to make promises that everybody knew he wasn't any good at keeping.

He pulled into the driveway and forced himself not to hurry up the front walk. He needed to ignore all these fatal yearnings, burn any bridges that might lead to her heart.

The key turned easily in the lock on the front door. Before pushing it open, he braced himself for the delicate scent, the Katie scent, that he knew lay beyond. The door swung open. *Bam.*

He breathed in the inevitable gulp, let it run through him. *Get over it, Cooper,* he thought, deliberately inhaling again. It's just another feminine perfume.

But it was *Katie's* perfume, and suddenly, he wanted to see her. Just one look, and he would be able to go on with the rest of the evening—scrounge up some dinner and then pull open the old briefcase.

She wasn't in the house. He wandered to the kitchen, through the dining room, peered into the open door of her bedroom. No Katie.

Back in the kitchen, he found a bottle of beer and flipped off the top. No note from her anywhere.

None of your business, Cooper.

Hadn't he turned his back on the husband role? What he should do was make a sandwich, finish his beer, and go over the report from Accounting.

Except the roast beef, rye bread and crispy lettuce all tasted wilted without Katie in the house. If he just knew where she was, he could be comfortable and get right to work.

Work. He slapped his palm to his forehead and hurried toward the back door. Yep. Lights blazed in the candy kitchen at the far side of the backyard. She'd said she had a lot of work to do today.

He pulled open the back door and strode into the cricket-calling darkness. Once he reassured himself she was doing fine, he would go right back to the house and his briefcase.

The smell of the candy kitchen was Katie and chocolate. He stood in the threshold, taking in the spare and clean white-tiled room. Countertops, a sink, a range and oven bordered one wall, a wide fridge and long worktable another, with a floral couch to the right of the door.

Katie, her hair gleaming in the fluorescent light, sat at the worktable, concentrating on something between her hands.

"Hi," Seth said, unsure whether she knew he was there.

She kept her head bent. "Hi."

He could go now. She was okay and the Accounting report was calling his name. "Smells good in here," he said, instead of leaving.

"That's candy for you."

Okay, so he wanted to look into her face before starting on that report. But the blond swing of her hair hid everything except the small tilt of her nose, and suddenly his eyesight wasn't so keen from this distance. "Rest of your day go okay?"

"Fine." With an experienced toss of her head, she whipped her hair away from her cheek and looked his way. "Yours?"

Seth found himself stepping into the room when he should have been stepping out of it. "You look tired."

She grimaced, her delicious lips twisting. "I have to wrap these chocolates for a delivery tomorrow." Her hair swung back to hide her face. "About seventy-five boxes to go."

"Can't you take a break?" He could tell she needed a cup of tea or a piece of her own chocolate.

She shook her head. "I need to finish before I go to bed tonight. Bet you brought work home, too."

The Accounting report immediately heightened its clamor. Seth ignored it. "Naw. Not really. Could I help you finish?"

She flashed him a tired smile. He advanced five more steps into the room. "I'm not sure you'd consider what I'm doing a manly job," she said.

He wasn't even listening. At this range he could see the purple shadows beneath her eyes. He didn't like them.

Beside her at the worktable he disliked what was left to do even more. Tiny boxes, each containing three chocolates, scattered the table's surface. As he watched Katie work, she expertly folded closed a small carton, sealed it with a Katie's Candies sticker, then decorated the box with purple ribbon and a little spray of silk flowers.

"Think you can do a few?" There was doubt *and* laughter in her eyes.

He looked down at his hands. They suddenly seemed jolly, green, and made up entirely of thumbs. "Of course I can," he lied. She looked so tired that he would try pirouetting if it would get her back to the house any sooner.

He probably was better at pirouetting. After a few false starts, they hit upon a workable plan. He closed the little boxes and stickered them, and she did the more delicate work of tying bows.

After a few minutes he settled into a rhythm and

his mind could wander beyond left flap, right flap, center flap, sticker. He became aware of Katie's shoulder, inches from his, and his gaze sidled her way to notice a spray of chocolate-covered drops on the front of her oversize shirt. "Looks like you need to wear an apron," he said.

She looked up, puzzled, then followed his gaze. "Oh, just me being messy." Her hand self-consciously brushed at the drops, unknowingly pressing the soft fabric against her breasts.

They're fuller. He tried to hide from the thought, but despite the prissiness of the work he was doing at the moment, he was a guy, and guys noticed things like that. Just in the few weeks he'd been with Katie, her breasts had gotten larger.

Did that mean they were more sensitive, too?

Shut up, Cooper.

He edged his chair away from her, and keeping his eyes to himself, commanded his fingers to work faster.

Unexpectedly, she touched the top of his hand, and his entire body, from head to toe, froze. He shouldn't look her way, so he kept his gaze strictly on the yellow box he was in the midst of constructing.

"Thanks," she said.

She left her fingers on his skin, so he resorted to counting boxes to keep his mind off the streaks of heat that rushed up his arm. *It would be dangerous to get close to her.*

Fifty-two boxes to go. She removed her hand, and

then in a rush, leaned toward him and kissed his cheek.

Crunch. The box flattened beneath his fingers. He whipped his face toward her and, startled, she drew back. *Damn. And thank goodness.* Without her movement they would have been lip-to-lip.

"Thanks," she said again. "For your help."

"My pleasure," he returned, but ruefully held up the demolished box. "And I hope you have a few extra."

He made the mistake of looking into her eyes. The shadows below them made them appear darker, more mysterious.

Breath came too slowly into his lungs. Problem was, he knew her mysteries. Every day in her company, every phone call, every breath of her fragrance told him about the kind of woman she was. Generous. Sweet.

Vulnerable.

She drew in a slow breath, too, and his gaze slid back down her body. *And don't forget desirable, Cooper.*

"Maybe..." He should go inside before he did something regrettable. Something unforgettable.

"Maybe we could talk about baby names," she said.

Seth blinked.

She smiled. "It will pass the time."

Reading the report from Accounting would pass the time. Talking about babies and baby names could only strengthen the ties between them. He inched his chair away from the table. "I—"

"I thought about Francis and Gabriel," she said.

The legs of Seth's chair screeched as he reversed direction and scraped it implacably toward her. "Pardon me?"

"Francis and Gabriel. Those are boys' names, of course. The twins could be girls."

"Francis and Gabriel are the names of angels or priests or something," he said with disbelief.

She nodded.

"No boy of mine will have a wussy name like that."

A saintly smile lit her face, the glow almost washing away the fatigue. "Okay, so what *do* you like?"

He frowned. "Bart, maybe? Max?"

Katie groaned. "No way. Uh-uh."

The fifty-two boxes came together quickly after that. No Francis, Gabriel, Bart or Max. Out-and-out refusal on Jason, Stephan or Dixon. They were just about to start ruling out god-awful girls' names when they finished.

Still aware of her long day, Seth hustled her out of the kitchen as soon as possible and back to the house. Their shoulders bumped companionably as they passed through the back door.

She yawned hugely. "I'm beat."

He walked her down the hall to her room and they both hesitated outside the door. "Good night," he said, and allowed himself to tuck her hair behind her ear.

She shivered, but he pretended not to notice. "We didn't get to those girl names," she said.

"Baby names." He shook his head in amazement. "Who would have thought such a thing would ever cross my mind?"

She leaned back against the doorjamb and looked up at him whimsically. "What did you see for your future, Seth? If you didn't want to be a father and husband?"

This wasn't the kind of discussion he liked. He should joke his way out, or walk his way out—*something*. But she held him there with the pretty strands of her hair, the glint of her eyes, the wet gleam of her mouth in the dim light of the hall. "I think I saw myself as...unencumbered. Unconnected," he answered absently, still mesmerized by her face. "Safely away."

Her arching brows moved toward each other. "Safely away?" she echoed.

"Did I say that?" He hadn't, had he?

She licked her lips. "You did."

And so what? The words didn't mean anything. Not like the meaning her mouth had for him right now. He leaned closer, watched those beautiful, full breasts rise against her shirt as she inhaled a breath.

And then, without premeditation, he closed the gap between them with a kiss, opening her mouth wide with the hard and hungry pressure of his mouth. She melted back against the wall and drew him toward her with clutching hands.

Need seared him, sending throbbing blood to his groin to make him instantly, achingly, aroused.

Connections. They were all around him. Marriage, baby names, her hands pulling him closer so that his chest rubbed the softness of her.

"Katie." The word came out desperate and low and he left her mouth and trailed his lips along her cheek to her jaw.

She moaned—the sound turning him on like nothing he could think of—and he bit her ear and dampened the shivers that slid down her neck with his tongue.

She wriggled against him, and he swore he felt the stiff points of her nipples through both their shirts.

He lifted his head and gulped in air. "Maybe we should talk about names again." He couldn't let her go just yet, but he shouldn't keep on kissing her.

She wriggled against him again, and his knee, all on its own, found a warm spot between her thighs. He pushed upward, and she gave that moan again. "Okay," she said. "Arnold, Abel, Archimedes."

He groaned and kissed the silliness away. As his tongue stroked hers, he slid one hand beneath her long shirt, over the sweet roundness of her pregnancy, to her breast.

Her head fell back and she pressed upward into his palm. "Oh, Seth. I can't tell you— You wouldn't believe..."

He liked the sound of that and drew his other hand under her shirt to cup both breasts. His thumbs circled the hard nipples through her bra.

She started whispering.

"What, honey?" he asked. "I can't hear you."

"Bertram, Bernie, Barney," she said, her eyes squeezed tightly shut. "I need to think of something else because this feels way too good."

"No such thing." And no way could he stop touching her. He fumbled with the front clasp of the bra and the hot fullness of her breasts tumbled into his palms.

She cried out.

He stilled. "Am I hurting you?"

She pressed into his hands. "You wouldn't believe..." she said again.

But he saw what his touch was doing to her. Even in the dim light, he could see her face was flushed and her breath ragged. He flexed his fingers into the soft skin and rubbed the center of his palms against her nipples. She cried out again, but now he recognized it as desiring and needy.

His heart slammed against his ribs and he pushed his thigh higher toward the juncture of hers. Her breath came faster now, and he plucked at her nipples, watching her face with awe as she swiftly and gloriously approached climax.

He wanted to see it. He had to watch what his touch could do to her. With slow, deliberate movements, he leaned into her, firmly pressing his leg higher, firmly pinching her nipples.

With a soft, almost hushed cry, she climaxed. Her cheeks flushed darker, her body tensed, then pushed back against his leg.

He felt her heat, her release, and the irrepressible, irrevocable sense of one more tie being strengthened.

7

Katie looked up at Seth's face and he saw that she recognized his instant regret.

Color surged to her cheeks. She shrank back against the cold plaster wall, twisting a bit to get away from the touch of his hands. She broke their linked gazes.

Sighing, he took one step back, his arms falling to his sides. "That was..."

"A mistake," Katie said quickly.

He grimaced. "'Incredible' was more what I had in mind." Though unwise.

The color on her face darkened. "These hormones..."

"Absolutely incredible." A ghost of a grin picked up the corners of his mouth.

Katie crossed her arms over her chest. "But." She said the word for him.

He shoved his hands into his pockets. "Yeah. But."

The grandfather clock in the hall ticked loudly in the growing silence. Katie's gaze darted to it, as if she wished she could open the little door in its base and disappear among the chimes.

She bit her lip. "I was feeling close to you." She spoke quietly, as if talking to herself. "Working with you... Baby names..."

"But I can't stop remembering how you looked asleep," he said abruptly.

Katie frowned. "What are you talking about?"

He raked his hands through his hair, then shoved them back into his pockets. "Look, Katie. I want—" He broke off, sighed. "What do *you* want, Katie?"

"To know you."

Fear took a stab at Seth's solar plexus and he winced. "I don't want to hurt you," he said. He watched the alert wariness sharpen in her eyes.

"You've said that before," she said. "Will you?"

Smart woman. Check first. Find out. Be very careful. Don't give away your heart before you know what kind of person it's going to.

He lifted his hand and stroked one of her cheekbones with his thumb. Then he forced his fingers away. "I might hurt you. I could."

"Will you?" she asked again.

How could he know? He still couldn't rid himself of that image of her a week ago, the one he'd been hiding from for days. Katie asleep, her head pillowed on her arms, waiting for him. A long breath didn't ease the tightness in his chest. "I want to be a father for Ryan's children. I hope I do live up to that. But anything else..."

"You don't want to be a husband?" Tension shimmered off her.

He averted his eyes from her face. "I don't know if I can." Did his genes, his childhood experience, doom him to failure?

Silence smothered the air in the hallway. Finally, Katie heaved her own sigh. "Then we'll just be a mother and a father."

He looked at her now, saw the set of her jaw, the firm line her just-kissed lips had become. He missed their softness, damn him.

"Good night, Seth." As she turned toward her room, he saw that she could even transform the firm line into a smile. A thin, I-won't-give-an-inch smile.

I'm doing the right thing, Seth told himself for the nine-hundreth time. Keeping this marriage in name only was safer. For Katie.

And feeling noble and righteous about it came pretty easily at the office or driving away from the house. The damn doubts only showed up at times like now, when he was headed home.

To make matters worse, he would probably see her there, too. This was 10:00 a.m., not 10 *p.m.*—the hour he usually made it home these days. But he'd forgotten an important file back at the house. With two meetings scheduled for this afternoon, he needed both the file and the notes he'd made.

Music pouring from the car speakers, Seth exited the freeway. Then something about the singer's heartbreak voice made his mind slide from business back to Katie again.

Just as in his nightly dreams, he saw her. Blond hair curving toward her lips. Her face flushed, her eyes darkening with passion. Beneath his hands, her skin—

Damn. He hastily overlaid the groin-tightening image with the other one that haunted him—Katie's sleek hair spilling over her arms as she pillowed her head, blue eyes closed in sleep as she waited for him.

Just remembering caused his heart to shudder, reminded him that he never wanted her to be hurt.

A familiar figure walking north a few miles from the house caught his attention.

He never expected to find Katie walking this far from home.

He swerved to the side of the road and used the button to unroll the passenger window. "What are you doing?" he yelled out the opening.

She peered at him through the window and frowned. She did that a lot lately. "Walking," she said.

"Where? Why?"

"Doctor's appointment." She took a step as if she meant to go on.

"Wait a minute." He noticed she wore a pair of black leggings, an oversize white shirt he'd never seen her wear before and shiny black penny loafers. Not really walking attire. "You're not driving? How far is the doctor's office?"

The frown hadn't let up. "Car broke down. And the office is far enough away that I need to hurry so I won't be late."

Unreasonable anger tightened Seth's grip on the steering wheel. "What do you mean your car broke down?" His voice came out harsh.

"I mean it broke down. Stopped moving. No more vroom-vroom-vroom." She started striding away.

Seth yanked the car into reverse and gave it enough gas to keep up with her. "You should have called me. Why didn't you call me? Where was Izzy? If she wasn't there, why didn't you call me?"

She sent him a sidelong look, but didn't stop moving. "I can handle it, Seth."

Still going backward, he had to swerve around a parked car to keep pace with her. "Get in," he yelled, once he made it close to the sidewalk again.

She shook her head and flapped her hand. "I'm fine. I'm fine."

Seth ground his teeth. He slammed on the brakes, jumped out of the car and dashed to the sidewalk. Even her elbow felt prickly, cupped in his palm. "Come on, let me give you a ride."

"I'm really fine, Seth. I know you're very busy and women take care of their broken-down cars, not to mention themselves, all the time."

That did it. The women-taking-care-of-themselves crack really got his temperature up. Gently, but with no room for negotiating, he directed her to the car and solicitously helped her in. He drove along feeling truckloads of burning guilt as he silently admitted that he'd been burying so much of himself in work that she probably felt she *couldn't* ask for his help.

Fine husband he had turned out to be. *I mean, just father of her children.*

Oh, hell, whatever.

At the doctor's office, Katie tried hopping out of the car while it was still moving. But Seth resorted to yelling again, and then insisted on parking the Explorer and walking with her to the elevator at the bottom of the six-story building.

She didn't want his company.

Ever since their...intimate encounter the week before, she'd done her best to steer clear of him. More than a husband, she wanted a father for the twins, and she was afraid that if she pressured him, he would back away from that, too.

Take off for parts unknown again.

She'd resolved to keep her distance, and his escorting her to the doctor's just seemed so...close.

A slew of people stepped into the elevator before her. She squeezed in at the front and wiggled her fingers in relieved farewell to Seth. As the door slid shut, a huge hand came out to stop its progress.

Seth crowded into the elevator beside her.

Katie squeezed her shoulders together to keep from pressing against him. "What are you doing? Don't you have to get back to work?"

He ran a hand through his shaggy hair. "I've got

to get you home, don't I? I'll call Grace and tell her to expect me when she sees me.''

That turned out to be a good idea. Once they reached the office on the fifth floor, the receptionist said the doctor was at the hospital finishing a delivery but wanted the patients to wait. Katie settled in a chair, doing her best to ignore Seth as he prowled the room, inspecting the aquarium, the view from the windows, and finally the center table stacked with magazines on women's issues and baby care.

Katie looked up from her book when he sprawled into the chair beside her. ''Why don't you go? I'll call Izzy or something.''

He scowled at her. ''If you couldn't call her an hour ago, how can you call her now?'' His fingers shuffled restlessly through the pages of the magazine he'd brought to his seat. ''God!''

''What?'' She peered over his shoulder. The magazine was open at a glossy spread of pictures chronicling a baby's birth from crowning—just its head appearing from the mother—to the crying, naked baby—umbilical cord still attached—being held in the doctor's hands.

''*God,*'' Seth said again.

Nerves tingled along Katie's spine. ''Yeah,'' she said, and leaned across him to hurriedly turn the page. *There.* Baby all snuggled in a cap and blanket, its mother in a fresh nightgown and looking like she was ready for breakfast in bed.

"Waitaminute." Seth flipped the page back. "God."

She wished he would stop saying that. She wished she knew if the expression he wore was merely fascination, or *horrid* fascination.

"Katie Cooper." The nurse called her name from the doorway to the examining rooms.

Katie rose, and in a quick move, snatched the magazine from Seth's hands. "I'll need something to read," she said, stuffing her paperback into her purse. If she wanted Seth's cooperation, it seemed smart to keep the more intimate—grittier—details of babies and childbirth to herself for the time being.

"Was that your husband?" The white-pantsuited woman led the way past the receptionist's desk.

"Uh-hmm."

The nurse turned back with a smile. "Pretty cute. You don't want him along?"

"No!" Katie stepped onto the scale, cruelly set up in the very public, forked crossroads of the examining rooms. She forced her voice lower. "No, thank you."

The woman smiled again, this time with sympathetic understanding. "One of *those,* hmm? Wants to believe the two of you will come home from a 49ers game and find that someone has delivered the baby—ready to play short-stop by spring—on the doorstep?"

Katie half smiled. If only Seth wanted a short-stop by spring. If only she could be sure Seth would still be here by spring. Ever since their conversation last week, she'd begun to wonder.

Scale hurdle cleared, the woman showed Katie into an examining room with a bed, a small sink, and a cartload of equipment that Katie had seen before. "Another sonogram?"

The nurse nodded. "Just routine. I should warn you, though. It's probably too early, but Dr. Simons loves to do his best at guessing the sex of the baby. Do you want to know?"

Katie vehemently shook her head. "I want to be surprised."

The nurse made a notation on her chart. "The doctor will be in soon."

Katie knew an OB-GYN's definition of "soon" and settled back on the examining table for a comfortable wait. She tossed the magazine on the countertop and dug out her paperback to return to her reading.

Two chapters flew by before the door swung open again. Jovial, cold-fingered Dr. Simons shook her hand, and then turned back to the doorway. "Look who I saw was loitering out there. He said he wants to see the babies."

Seth stepped hesitantly into the room.

Oh, no. She didn't want him with her now. It would seem too...personal. The last time she'd gotten *personal* with him, she'd ended up embarrassed and rebuffed. "You don't have to," she said, clutching her book tightly.

He slid a glance around the room and let it linger on the cart of equipment. "It looks sort of interesting."

"To say the least," Dr. Simons boomed. "Wait until you see what's going on *inside* Mrs. Cooper. Now that's really interesting."

Seth seemed to solidify in the doorway, and Katie sighed as another nurse bustled into the room, shoving him a little forward so the door could be shut. He ended up by the top of the examination table, behind her head, as the nurse pushed up Katie's shirt and inched down her leggings to reveal the roundness of her abdomen.

Katie felt her face burn as she imagined Seth's view of her pregnant body.

His breath washed over her ear. "Pretty cute little belly," he whispered. His hand stroked her hair back off her forehead. "I like it."

Katie warmed again, but not with embarrassment this time. "Thank you," she said quietly, knowing he'd read her discomfort and tried to ease it.

Shivers ran over her skin as the nurse spread the cold jelly over her stomach.

"What's that for?" Seth asked.

"Improves the reception," the nurse answered, nodding at the screen the doctor had flipped on. "Like cable instead of rabbit ears."

Another shiver rippled through Katie. The room was cold, the jelly was cold, and her nerves seemed to rattle around in her body. What would Seth think of seeing inside her womb, of seeing the babies for the very first time?

She licked her dry lips and tilted her head to see his face. "Why don't you go now," she said urgently. "I don't want you to see—"

"Show time!" Dr. Simons's voice boomed again. In her agitation, Katie hadn't even registered the touch of the sonogram's wand to her skin.

With her gaze on Seth's face, she saw his response to his first glimpse of the babies. As Dr. Simons pointed at the fuzzy image to trace the chambers of their hearts, their limbs, the shapes of their heads and feet, Seth's face stilled. But his hand traveled from her hair to her shoulder, to her fingers. He laced his with hers.

His warmth and strength flowed into her arm as the doctor continued the examination. Katie turned her gaze from Seth to the screen, her breath catching as a tiny foot moved, or a hand fluttered. *Hello again, sweethearts.* And the fuzzy images touched her even more because she was sharing them with someone, someone joined biologically to the babies.

Someone joined, hand to hand, with her.

When Dr. Simons pronounced the babies healthy and the pregnancy going fine, Seth's grip tightened. But his face remained unreadable.

Katie didn't know what their clasped hands meant. She couldn't interpret the gravelly grunts he emitted in response to the doctor's good-humored comments.

When Dr. Simons finally turned off the monitor, she had no idea what the long sigh Seth released meant.

She only knew that the man she wanted to keep her distance from had looked inside her body.

And the intimacy that wrought made her want to barricade her soul.

After they left the doctor's office, Seth didn't seem to want to go back to work. He insisted on taking Katie to lunch, then for a drive. He stopped to make another phone call to Grace, but he refused to discuss work or anything else relevant to the office.

The afternoon wasn't silent, however. He talked a lot about places he'd been, about Ryan as a young boy, about books and teachers and music. She learned more about him in one afternoon than she had in all the weeks they'd lived together.

But she had the feeling he was hiding something all the same. And she was pretty certain it was something about the babies.

Around 4:00 p.m. he stopped at the local mall. He said he wanted to pick up some CDs, update his collection after being out of the country for so many months.

But he bypassed two music stores without explanation. Tension infused Katie with each store he prowled past. It was obvious he wanted something, or wanted to tell her something. Were the babies too real for him now, too? Would he walk out as Tom had done? The fear she'd suppressed every day since she'd agreed to marry Seth welled up inside her.

Suddenly he grasped her hand and dragged her through the doors of a shop. She had only an instant to read the name of the place: Bundles of Joy.

"Start grabbing," he said.

"What?" Katie stood dumbfounded as he tucked two baby blankets, two stuffed sheep, and two tiny sleepers under his arm.

A bemused-looking salesclerk hurried toward them. "Can I help you, sir? Ma'am?"

Seth nodded and transferred the items he'd selected to the clerk's empty hands. "We need two of everything. Twins. Don't let me walk out of here with just one of something."

"Well, certainly, sir, and congratulations." The clerk headed toward the counter.

Seth swung toward Katie. "Why are you just standing there?"

Katie blinked. "I don't know. I don't know what I'm supposed to be doing."

He frowned. "Buying stuff for the babies."

Another trickle of nervousness ran down Katie's spine like a tear. *Was he buying things for them, stocking up the nursery, in order to pave the way for leaving?*

"You haven't told me what you thought about... the babies," Katie said. Beside her, he cocked his head as he stared at a row of pillows, half shaped like elephants, half shaped like hippos. Real tears stung the corners of her eyes.

Seth looked her way and his eyes narrowed. "You're not crying?" he asked softly.

She blinked. "Of course not."

His hand came toward her, dropped. "Good. Because we need a lot more. Do you want to pick out double sets of towels, or should I?"

Katie blinked again. "I guess I will."

He nodded and walked away a few steps, then turned back. "And pacifiers. I think someone in there was sucking their thumb. No Cooper kid better do that."

Despite herself, Katie had to grin. Apparently Coopers weren't thumb-suckers.

Upon leaving the store, Seth carried all the bags himself. Clothes, blankets, towels, soft toys—a whole jumble of stuff in white, soft yellow and mint green. Once they reached home, he insisted on hauling it all to the third bedroom, which Katie planned to use as the nursery.

He still hadn't said anything about the sonogram. She still wondered if he'd bought the stuff as a way to buy off his conscience if he left. And looking at the pile in the middle of the carpet, Katie knew she had to find out the truth.

"So what's this about?" she said, gesturing at the small mountain of goodies. "What does all this mean?"

Seth stared at her, and she could feel that betraying sting of tears again. "You *are* crying. Why?"

Katie tried gulping back the lump in her throat. "Because I don't know how you feel. Now that you've seen the babies. I don't know why you bought these things."

"Well..." In the glow from the soft dome light, Katie thought she saw his face reddening. He quickly bent over to retrieve two of the soft toys that had tumbled from a bag. A squishy gray terry-cloth elephant and a stegosaurus in yellow velour. His gaze stayed on the little animals. "They're real to me now."

"The elephant and the dinosaur?" Katie knew he didn't mean them at all, but she was afraid that he'd said all he was planning to.

He didn't laugh. "The babies are real to me now. Your babies."

That still didn't tell her what she wanted to know. But before she could ask, his head lifted, and his green eyes—dark, dark like a fantasy forest—stared into hers. "Our babies," he said.

Katie's heart took a twisty slide toward her stomach. "Oh, Seth."

And she didn't know how she got there or who had moved first, but in the next pulse-beat she was in his arms, her cheek pressed against his chest, a soft elephant trunk tickling her chin.

His heart pounded in her ear and she sighed. *Seth was here. Seth was with her.*

"They're beautiful, aren't they?" she asked.

His smile warmed his voice. "The elephant and the dinosaur?"

She pushed a bit away from his chest and grinned up at him. "No, silly. Our babies. They're beautiful."

The smile died on his face. His eyes darkened to that thrilling, primeval green. Katie's heart slid again—*whooshed*, actually.

"No, silly," Seth repeated in a hoarse whisper. "*You're* beautiful. Inside and out."

8

————➤ ◄————

With Katie in his arms, Seth tried getting hold of his tumbling emotions, as well. Elation skittered away. Scared witless was here and gone. Uncertainty lasted briefly in his clutches. He was left feeling only absolutely sure.

Absolutely sure that despite and because of everything he'd seen today, he was going to make love to Katie.

If she would have him.

Her mouth said yes. Not in a word, but in the way it turned up to his and then opened at the slightest possible pressure.

Her warm breath puffed over his lips, and he savored the sensation by brushing each corner of her mouth, putting off the moment he would touch her with his tongue.

Her eyes drifted shut, and he stared down at her face. Eyelashes like fairy fringe. Tiny bodies growing inside her womb. Miracles, both.

"Katie," he whispered.

Eyes still shut, she smiled, apparently hearing something she liked in his voice. "Yes."

Yes. A fine tremor shook his hands and he cupped her face to still their movement. Hungry for her now, he took her mouth, pushed into it with his tongue. Another tremor ran down his spine and slid over his thighs, filling him with pure male desire.

His tongue plunged again. She tasted like heat, and she squirmed against him, her breasts rubbing his chest. He wanted to touch them again, to watch her find satisfaction with his hands on her. Then he wanted more. He wanted to be inside her. He wanted to be *with* her.

She ran her hands up his back. More tremors. Then she slid her nails along his spine. He pushed into her mouth again with his tongue.

Her hands moved around him and came between their bodies to fumble with the buttons of his shirt. He groaned.

"Bad?" A laugh was in her voice.

"Beauty—" A button released and he lost his breath. He grabbed her fingers. "Slower," he said.

She slipped her hands from his and moved down to the next button. An instant more, then she spread the sides of his shirt, her knuckles brushing against his ribs. "Beauty..." His protest trailed off as she laid her face against him.

His heart beat against her cheek. Her breath seared his skin, tightening his chest, making him ache. Oh, hell. Maybe he would die before he found his way inside her.

Her face turned and her mouth opened wetly against the skin over his heart.

Dying was okay.

She looked up at him then, eyes smoky dark, the blue almost obscured by her pupils. "I want you, Seth."

No, dying was great. "You'll have me, Katie."

He felt a shudder roll through her at the promise, and then he had to taste her again, had to have her mouth under his and her tongue mingling with his tongue. He stroked the soft heat of her mouth and heard her moan.

Her fingers splayed over his chest, fingernails biting lightly, erotically into him. Impatient, he didn't even try for the buttons of her shirt, but reached for the hem and drew the garment over her head.

He stared at what he'd revealed. At what he'd touched but never seen. Full breasts in a utilitarian white bra. Very little of her skin showed, but that it was *her* skin, Katie's skin, the sight became as much of a turn-on as if she wore the skimpiest scrap of lace.

His hands started shaking again. Katie had a funny look on her face, as if she might be second-guessing her decision, or him, or both. He clenched his fingers into fists at his sides and looked into her face. "Are you okay? Are you sure?"

The pink on her cheekbones darkened. She absently ran a thumb over his nipple, hardening it, and he had to suck in a quick breath. "It's just...my body..." she began.

So that was it. "Turns me on, Katie. I don't know what it was like before the babies, but let me tell you, what I see now makes me feel eighteen again."

She smiled, that quirky dimple she had peeking out. "Eighteen?" She sounded kind of pleased with herself.

He grinned ruefully. "Uh, I hate to break it to you, Beauty, but that's not necessarily a good thing. We're gonna have to go slow."

All the doubts seemed to have left her. She picked up one of his hands and brought it to her mouth. "Tell that to my hormones." She kissed his palm, then lightly bit the pad of his thumb.

His heart rocketed against his ribs. "That's it," he choked out. That was all the warning she was going to get, too. He didn't have the willpower for any more talk, for anything less than his hands upon her skin.

The clasp at the back of her bra gave way easily, and he tore the material away from her breasts. And there they were for him—creamy, with stiff, dark-raspberry crowns that he had to taste. Now.

Her skin was smooth against his cheeks and he brushed over her breasts with his beard. And then again, because he could tell from her gasp and her clutching fingers that she wanted more of the sensation. Finally, just for him, he took a nipple into his mouth, rolling it around his tongue, then sucking.

Maybe he had died after all. And heaven—or

hell—was a place where his every nerve screamed its awareness of her, from the shaggy ends of his hair tickling her neck to the hardness of his knee pressed against the softness of her thigh. He sucked harder, because he wanted her more, and felt her moan and her muscles tense.

So hot. So incredibly hot. He brought his hand to her other breast, cupped it in his palm, knowing he would satisfy her in moments. Loving the idea of it.

But she had ideas herself. "Seth." She spoke urgently, in a gasping rush. "Please, Seth. You, too."

Her hands moved to his belt. "Please Seth. Me and you."

He drew his head away from her breast. "I like it this way. I like watching you. Making it happen."

"Make it happen for both of us." Her hands unfastened the buckle.

The skin at his waist goose-bumped and the searing chills traveled toward his heart and his groin. But he didn't want her like this. Not here. "Let's go to the bedroom, Katie."

Maybe his heavy breathing was affecting her hearing, because she didn't move. Her hands kept busy, though, sliding inside his boxers to cup him.

Her touch sped like a flaming arrow through him. "Katie." He gasped, trying to bring air and sense back to his body. "Katie. The bedroom."

She leaned into him, the smooth skin of her breasts pressing against his chest, her mouth on his neck, her hands exploring him.

He had to slow this down. Think of the bedroom, the cool length of the hall, the cool sheets. He grabbed her wrist and gritted his teeth as he pulled her sweet touch away from his skin. "The bedroom," he said firmly. She lifted her shirt from the floor and held it against her as he drew her with him toward the place where he slept.

She pulled back as they almost passed the doorway of her own room. He looked down at her, her eyes luminous with passion. "Bigger bed," she said simply.

He smiled, and ran his thumb over her lips. "But the, uh, necessaries, are in my room."

Her brow furrowed. " 'Necessaries'?"

"Uh, you know, protection."

"Protection from what? If it's pregnancy you're worried about—" that impish dimple of hers popped out "—it's a little too late."

Seth froze, then felt another rush of hot chills over his skin. "Oh. Of course. It's just, I've never been with a woman without...something between us."

She was already backing into her room. "This way," she said, leading him to the bed.

It was a blur of skin and kisses after that. Seth knew he made Katie moan, could feel it through her skin, but the pounding of his heartbeat in his ears was the only accompaniment he could hear as he bared each inch of her body, touched it, tasted it, then let his be touched and tasted, too.

He never lost contact with her as they twined and

intertwined on the sheets, never letting an instant pass without touching her—a hand on her thigh, the brush of his hair against her belly, his tongue along her neck. He couldn't give up the connection, not even when she parted her thighs so willingly and begged him to come inside her with the hottest kiss he'd ever tasted.

He positioned himself over her, his hand gently cupping the juncture of her thighs, pushing her open wider so his legs could fit between hers. Gritting his teeth, he allowed himself just to brush against her soft, wet heat, and the feel of skin on skin made him dizzy.

He joined to her then, inch by inch, her sweet heat enclosing him, binding him to her.

Once inside her, he thought for sure he would never be able to leave, but the clasp of her thighs around his waist spurred him to move—almost withdrawing, but not quite; sinking back in, almost withdrawing again.

Never leaving entirely. Never that. No.

Just a rhythm of passion that he heard in his heartbeat, read on her face, felt in the hot, hot pool of her kiss.

She moved against him, with him, bonding him to her with her legs, her hands, the femininity of her that he'd never been so intimate with before.

A net of raw passion dropped over him, moving him forward, forward, into her. Into her again, higher, until she quivered around him and cried out, and then he pushed into her one more time and found his own release.

Release. Could he call it that? he wondered, leaning on his elbows and struggling to find his breath. Because he didn't feel released. In Katie's beautiful face, in the warm, pulsing place of her body, he'd found bondage.

And most confusing, the fetters didn't hurt at all.

It was fully dark in her bedroom and Katie felt as if their lovemaking had gone on for hours. She ran her hand lightly over Seth's forearm, which was tucked around her, between her breasts and her rounding belly.

He breathed heavily against her ear, the slow breaths rhythmically washing chills across her ultra-sensitized skin. The warmth of his spooning body cradled her, and she closed her eyes in appreciation of the feeling.

Thank you, Seth. She whispered the words in her head, not wanting to disturb him. Even if he'd been awake she would have kept them to herself. Something told her Seth wouldn't thank *her* for her gratitude. But making love with him had been special.

Get real, girl. Okay, more than special. It had been almost sacred, like their marriage finally really meant something. Maybe they could be a family now.

Carefully, gently, so he wouldn't wake, Katie turned in Seth's embrace. She faced him across the pillow, her eyes so accustomed to the darkness now that she could make out the rugged features of his face.

With her gaze she traced the thick, stubby curve of his eyelashes, the bold slash of his nose, the erotic, full outline of his mouth. She could watch him all night, reliving the melting moments they'd had together just by watching the rise and fall of his chest.

A shiver overtook her just thinking about his hands on her. He'd whispered things against her skin, called her "Beauty," made her *feel* beautiful about her plumping body. As she stared at him, something inside her turned inside out. She felt her pulse begin to pound, an almost-painful drumbeat against her wrists, her throat, her chest.

What did it mean? What was her body trying to say? Was it—

But just when she thought she could pinpoint the feeling, Seth's eyes opened. He stared at her for a moment, and her pulse beats slowed in uneasiness.

One of his big palms grazed her hip, and ran up her side to her shoulder. He blinked. "Not a dream," he mumbled.

She started breathing again. "It's me."

His hand smoothed back down to her hip. "In the flesh." A sleepy, wicked grin kicked up the corners of his mouth.

His caressing hand made *her* feel wicked. Warmth rose up from her toes as he traced rough circles on the bare skin of her flank. Her nipples tightened immediately, and although the sheet was pushed down to her waist, she hoped he wouldn't notice.

"Mmm," he said in appreciation, but when she hastily met his gaze he was focused on her eyes.

"Mmm, what?" she asked, and surreptitiously caught the sheet between scissored fingers and started edging it toward her throat.

Just as casually, he slid it out of her grip. Then, as if she was a lightweight rag doll, he grasped her forearms and pulled her over on top of him. Her breasts brushed the hot skin of his chest, tightening the tips even more.

"Hey, that's manhandling!" she protested, her pulse notching up to that primitive beat again.

Another wicked grin. "I'll show you a man handle."

And she felt it, all right. He nudged her in the very place that already ached for him. "Oh, Seth." She heard the longing in her voice, worried about how vulnerable he could make her feel.

"Oh, Katie." He said the words back to her. With his hands tangled in her hair, he urged her head closer. "Let me kiss you, Beauty," he whispered.

And then he murmured against her lips, "Let me in," and his tongue entered her mouth and that other part of him entered the intimate heat of her body as if it couldn't bear to be separated from her.

He rocked gently into her and Katie felt the passion lifting her, taking her off the white cotton sheets to a plane of pleasure and closeness that she'd never shared with anyone in her entire life. As he pushed her higher with his hips, Katie climbed to a new level of understanding. For the first time, those nagging questions—Why me? Why Karen and Ryan? Why the pregnancy?—made some sort of grand, universal sense that she could almost, almost touch.

"Katie." Seth called to her urgently. "Honey, I'm there, I'm there. Come with me." His fingers found a special spot between her legs that made her cry out.

One more thrust and all the answers she'd felt so close to danced away in the winds of pure, strong pleasure.

Later, it was she who awoke to find him watching her. Her heart executed a slow tumble. There was a wariness in his eyes, something that had been missing since the moment they began to make love.

"What is it?" she whispered. She glanced at the clock—5:00 a.m.

"You scare me when you sleep." The words seemed wrenched from him, so raw that she knew they were the barest truth.

She tentatively touched his hair. "Why?"

He slid away from her, toward the edge of the bed. "So fragile…I could break you."

Katie clenched the sheet between her hands. "I'm fine, Seth. I won't break."

But he was out of the bed already and headed down the hall.

Seth called himself all kinds of names—coward and fool being the kindest of them—but gave excuses to Katie anyway as to why he spent the next two nights on the couch at his office.

He got up on the third morning, stiff and sore, telling himself it was fit punishment. Yeah, as he had told Katie, he'd missed an entire day of work when he'd taken her to that appointment, and yeah, the board was meeting at 10:00 a.m. today, but he hadn't stayed away from her because of work.

He'd stayed away out of fear.

The closer he came to Katie, the more he worried about the pain of abandonment. The kind of pain that first his father, then his mother had given to him and Ryan. The kind of pain he might make Katie suffer.

He didn't let himself listen to the little voice that said it might be too late.

For both of them.

His assistant Grace knocked lightly on the door, gave him one look, and then took pity on him. Within half an hour she'd had four *grande* cups of his favorite takeout coffee delivered, along with bagels and cream cheese.

By nine-thirty he felt human and even—surprise, surprise—adequately prepared for the board meeting. The entire staff had worked tirelessly to put together a seamless package that he hoped would satisfy the directors.

As he took his place at the long conference table, he even realized he'd enjoyed the challenge. Ryan's part of the business had been unfamiliar, but now that

Seth had it under control, he felt satisfaction in the work. He hadn't missed the travel for one instant.

Six hours and one catered lunch later, he sat alone in his same place at the conference table, shell-shocked.

"I did it, Ry," he said aloud to the empty room. He'd let the overworked staff go home early after the board gave their collective thumbs-up. "*We* did it." He'd felt his brother's presence today, like a hand on his shoulder, as he presented to the directors the re-organization plan and the projected earnings of some new ideas he wanted to put in place.

"They were so impressed with what we'd accomplished, Ry, that the news is even better." Seth flicked a paper clip across the table. "They don't object to Phyllis and Jared sharing your duties. That means I can go back to finding new products."

He flicked another paper clip, and it slid off the table onto the floor. "I've been thinking about Iceland."

Of course, Ryan didn't answer. He didn't have to. Seth knew that Ryan would hate the idea of Seth running out on Katie now. But she and the babies would still have the protection of his name, wouldn't they?

Seth ran his hands through his hair and slowly rose from his chair. He would bring up the idea to Katie and see what she had to say. Maybe it would make sense to her, too.

He found her in the kitchen at home, preparing what looked like a dinner for one. Without comment, she pulled another chicken breast from the freezer.

"What can I do?" he asked, hoping she wouldn't answer, *Go to hell.*

"Make the salad." She slid a cool look at him from her blue eyes, but the chill in her gaze couldn't make him forget the hot feel of her in his arms. He hadn't seen her in over forty-eight hours, but he'd thought of her forty-eight times an hour—the curve of her hip, the passionate sound of her moans, the taste of her on his tongue.

But with the looks she was giving him, she would probably be glad to see him leave.

"The board meeting went great," he offered into the silence.

A genuine smile briefly lit her face. "I know. I couldn't stand the suspense so I called Grace. I caught her right as she was leaving. She said the board feels the company's in good hands, even with Ryan gone."

He opened the refrigerator and stuck his head in. "She tell you anything else?"

"There's more?" Katie asked.

Seth left his head in the refrigerator. He needed cooling off around Katie anyhow. "Not much," he said, stalling. "How have the past couple of days been for you?"

"Lonely."

Seth straightened and shut the fridge door. "I'm sorry." With his gaze, he followed the curve of her hair to her jaw, just allowing himself a moment's contemplation of her mouth. "Forgive me."

She smiled again, warming him. "All's well that ends well. You made the board happy."

But can I ever make you *happy?* He took a long breath. "I'm afraid I'm a lot more like my father than I want to be, Katie." Maybe he could make her see. "He worked crazy hours. God, I hardly remember a time when he was at home, and then, just when Ryan and I needed a man in our lives, he walked out on Mom and us." And their mother had never recovered from the pain.

Katie's brow creased. "You're not your father, Seth."

How do you know? he wanted to ask. He wanted to demand how she could know he wouldn't hurt her and the babies.

He needed to tell her that he couldn't stay without giving her that guarantee. "Katie, I—" He tried out the rest of the sentence in his mind first. *I think it would be best if I left you.*

Suddenly she gasped and went completely still, as if she could read his mind. She gasped again, and looking down at her abdomen, moved one hand to cover it.

Seth's heart jumped. "What?" God, were his *thoughts* hurting her now? "What's the matter? Are you in pain?"

Her face lifted, and a beatific smile lit her face. Her eyes blazed at him, the bluest he'd ever seen them. "I felt them move," she said hoarsely. "I've seen them wriggling on the sonogram before, but I've never felt them." She looked down at her belly again, and then back up.

Her smile, unbelievably, grew more delighted. "Somebody's kicking me."

It was her delight that drew him. He crossed the few steps to her and cupped her cheek. "Do I need to give somebody a talking-to?" He couldn't help but smile, either.

She didn't answer, just took his hand and pressed it against the swell of her stomach. "See? See? There. Do you feel it?"

The warmth of her body crept into his palm. "Yeah, Beauty, I feel it," he lied.

With a silent chuckle, Katie entwined her fingers with Seth's. She could tell he was fibbing. But she loved him all the more for it.

Loved him all the more for it. The words echoed in her brain and her heart started a pounding climb toward her throat. *Oh, God.*

What she'd felt the other night when they'd been in bed, what had made what they'd done there seem sacred, was that she loved him. She loved Seth.

She swallowed, and with her free hand pushed the hair off his forehead. It was his habitual gesture, and one she always wanted to make for him. It was a wifely gesture. A loving gesture.

A gesture now hers to make.

"Seth..." Her voice was hoarser than before.

His gaze became concerned. "Are you in pain? Is their moving around supposed to hurt you like this?"

She shook her head. "I'm not in pain. I'm just...happy." Maybe she should tell him that she loved him. Maybe this was the right time.

He groaned. "I wish I knew more about this stuff."

She pushed back his hair again. "You're going to be just fine, Seth. A fine father."

Tension hardened his muscles. She could feel them stiffen, and she frowned. "You're not really worried about that, are you?"

He didn't answer.

She frowned deeper. "Do you want to talk about it?"

His hand flexed gently over her belly. "Not right now," he said.

Relieved, Katie smiled. "Good. Because I've missed you, and suddenly, there's something I want to do instead of talk."

She could tell Seth still felt tense. With his hand in hers, he followed slowly and stiffly as she led him from the kitchen down the hall. When she stopped at her bedroom, he seemed surprised.

"Don't you want to?" she asked, nervousness flickering through her.

He touched her cheek. "More than I could ever say."

"Then come to bed with me. I want to show you how I feel."

He didn't ask her how that was. She didn't tell him in words, but hoped he felt the truth in the way she welcomed him into her body.

9

Katie noticed the instant Izzy stopped chopping onions for the taco salad and began rubbing her back. "Hurting again?" she asked.

Izzy nodded. "Bothering me since yesterday. It's why I'm so glad you and Seth came over today. I needed the distraction."

So had Katie. A week had gone by since she'd realized she loved Seth, but she'd kept the knowledge to herself. Katie frowned as her friend continued rubbing. "But maybe Seth and I should go, Izzy." They'd been invited to the other couple's remote house in the coastal mountains for lunch and dinner.

Red curls bounced around Izzy's pale face as she shook her head. "Please don't. I'm not going to make it through the last four weeks of this pregnancy unless I have something else to think about. Tell me the latest about you and Seth."

Katie forced a smile onto her face. "Well, since you've been off, you missed the big excitement. The board is happy with Seth's reorganization. The company is safe and secure and pronounced A-okay by the board members.''

With a grimace, Izzy resumed chopping. "So how come Seth looks like someone's stretching him on the rack? You guys abstaining from sex again?"

"Izzy!" Katie craned her neck and looked out the window to be sure Dan and Seth were still tramping about the pine trees in the front yard. "Our sex life is fine, thank you very much."

Awesome was more like it. Every night Seth took her in his arms and made love to her with a tenderness and urgency that heated her blood—but somehow did nothing to reveal the state of his heart.

Izzy stopped chopping again. "Something's bothering you, too."

"I don't know what to do," Katie found herself blurting out. "I...I discovered I'm in love with Seth, but I don't know if I should tell him."

Instead of showing signs of astonishment or elation, as Katie expected, Izzy merely chuckled and kept on chopping. "No surprise there."

"'No surprise there'? What's that mean?"

Izzy looked up from the onion. "It means you're not stupid, Katie. And me, neither. There was something between you and Seth from the start. Do you think I would have let you marry some man you wouldn't fall in love with? Pu-leez."

Katie sputtered.

Izzy laughed. "You're getting red in the face."

Katie sputtered some more. "If you're so smart, Mrs. Isabelle Hughes, what do I do now?"

"You're worried about telling him?"

Katie nodded. "I'm afraid I'll scare him away. Or make him feel obligated to tell me something he doesn't feel."

Izzy shook her head. "Seth doesn't strike me as the kind of guy to make pity declarations."

"You're right." Katie sighed. "I'm just being a wimp. If I don't tell him how I feel, then he won't have to tell me how he *doesn't* feel."

"I *think* that makes sense." Izzy started rubbing her back again. "But you're going to have to get your guts up and talk to him. You gotta find out how he feels, Katie."

Find out how he feels. Katie held on to the thought as the two couples took a prelunch hike through the woods surrounding Dan and Izzy's home. When Izzy claimed she was tired and was going back to the house, Katie volunteered to accompany her.

The men waved, then kept walking. Izzy grumbled. "I was giving you an opportunity to get Seth alone," she said. "Dan could have come back with me."

Katie shivered, staring up at the sky. "Thanks, but it looks like rain. I'll talk to him later. On the way home."

"Wimp is right." Izzy shook her head, but then linked arms with Katie and slowed her walk. "But I like the company anyhow."

At the house, Katie suspected that Izzy had wanted

to return for a reason other than to give her and Seth time alone together. As soon as they reached the entryway, Izzy said she was going to lie down. Maybe even take a nap.

This was so unlike Izzy's normal frenetic energy, that Katie narrowed her gaze. "Are you okay? Do you want me to track down Dan?"

Izzy groaned. "No, no. Don't tell him a thing. He's been freaking out imagining all sorts of horrors. I'm worried about him making it in the delivery room."

Katie frowned. "I'm worried about you making it *to* the delivery room."

"Stop worrying," Izzy said. "I just want to lie down for a bit."

Katie settled her in the master bedroom with a warm blanket and the TV remote control. She left Izzy mumbling about "damn football" as she clicked from channel to channel.

Within minutes a light rain started. Katie looked out the back windows, a premonitory shiver rolling down her spine. Where were the men? The sky darkened. The rain beat harder against the roof. Katie shivered again.

She wanted to get Dan back to Izzy as soon as possible. She hurried through the door from the kitchen to the garage. Rain boots, umbrellas and waterproof ponchos hung on the far wall. The least she could do was meet the guys halfway with rain gear.

Her head was just poking through her own rain cape when she heard their voices. They were obviously outside, just on the other side of the wall. Katie sighed in relief and pulled the poncho back off.

"Congratulations on the board's approval, again, Seth," Dan was saying. "I knew you'd pull it off."

"I wish I'd known," Seth replied. "I would have done a bunch of things differently."

Katie stilled. The men had to be standing beneath the overhang of the roof and didn't seem to be in any hurry to come inside. She should call to them.

What were the "bunch of things" Seth would have done differently?

Find out how he feels. That admonition echoed in Katie's head. She stayed where she was, silent.

"What would you have done different?" It was Dan's voice.

Thank you, Dan, Katie thought. *I owe you a pound of my best chocolates.*

She imagined Seth's shrug. "I didn't tell you all of it. I haven't told anybody outside the company."

"What are you talking about?" Dan again.

"The board approved two of the VPs to take over Ryan's duties."

"Meaning what?" Dan asked.

"Meaning I could go back to my old job."

Katie couldn't hear Dan's response. Her heart started knocking so loudly that she could only listen to its panicked beat. *Back to my old job.* Seth could start wandering again. He would leave her and the babies behind. He would leave her without all she wanted for them. He would leave her without the love of her life.

She wanted to scream. She wanted to cry. She wanted to go find Izzy and tell her that she wasn't so smart after all.

The men were still talking. Katie's heart continued to drum in her ears like a high-school parade band, but their words floated into her head anyway.

"What are you going to do?" Dan asked.

"I've been thinking about Iceland."

Iceland? Katie bit her lip. In her opinion, he belonged in a much warmer place.

"But I don't know anything for sure," Seth continued. "First I've got to see Katie through the birth of the twins." There was what seemed like a gloomy pause. "Let's talk about something else."

Dan obligingly left the subject and started discussing the rain. "I don't know about this latest deluge," he said ominously. "The hills are already saturated from that big storm we had last week."

Certain she'd already heard the worst, Katie went back into the house to wait.

Seth removed his wet coat, left it on the front porch and followed Dan into the house. Katie met them immediately, her face pale and set. Her gaze flicked between the two men. "Dan, Izzy isn't feeling too well. Maybe you should go see how she's doing."

The color immediately slid from Dan's face. "God," he said, staring at Katie. "Really? God."

Katie stared pointedly at Dan's feet, which had seemed to take root in the plank floor. "Maybe God can get you to the bedroom, Dan. To check on Izzy."

Impossibly, Dan turned even paler.

Katie grabbed his arm and dragged him toward the hallway. *"Go."*

Robotlike, Dan walked toward the master bedroom.

Seth tried grinning at Katie in shared amusement, but her expression didn't relax. As a matter of fact, she looked like his reflection had looked in the mirror this past week. Tense. Torn. Uncertain as to the next step.

"What's the matter, Beauty?" The nickname slipped out, and she flinched as if it hurt her. Seth cleared his throat. "Are you worried about Izzy? What's the matter with her?"

"Her back's bothering her again and she's tired." Katie crossed her arms protectively over her abdomen. "Can I talk to you?"

"Sure." Seth knew already he wasn't going to like the conversation but he followed her to the living-room couch. "We might think about heading down the hill earlier than we planned. Dan says this much rain can mean trouble."

When he sat on the couch, she moved to the stuffed armchair opposite him. The tension hadn't left her face. "I think I might stay here tonight."

Seth frowned. "What? Are you that worried about Izzy?"

Katie bit her lip. "This isn't about Izzy. This is about me."

A cold finger traveled down Seth's spine. "What are you talking about?"

She bit her lip again.

Seth didn't like the gesture. He stood. "Let's go home, Katie. Izzy isn't feeling well, you seem nervous and Dan has worried me about the rain."

She shook her head slowly.

He didn't want to take that answer. The pound of the rain on the roof was as hard as his resolve to get Katie out of here. "I'm serious."

"Me, too," she said.

When she didn't move from her chair, Seth sat back down on the couch. He would listen to her quickly, *then* make her go.

"It began when I was a little girl."

Seth groaned inwardly. Was she going to hash over twenty years? The rain rattled in the gutter downspouts.

"Ever since then, somewhere inside, I've believed everything would have been perfect if my father had stayed."

Seth ran his hand through his hair. "Can we talk about this in the car?"

She shook her head adamantly and began tracing patterns with one finger on the arm of the chair. "If my father had stayed I felt nothing bad would ever have happened to me. No disappointments, no worries. If we had all stayed in the same house—a mommy, a daddy, Karen and me—nothing bad could have touched us. As a *family* we would have been protected from pain."

She looked up. "I even think that until this moment, I believed that if my parents hadn't broken up, Karen wouldn't have died."

Seth swallowed. There was pain now, written all over her face. He wanted to take her in his arms, but she looked away from him and watched her finger make ceaseless circles on the chair. "What made you change your mind?" he asked hoarsely.

"You. Or rather, the place I was assigning you in my life."

Seth swallowed again. "What place is that?"

"*Was* that," she corrected. "The daddy place, of course. The husband place. And that's how the twins and I would become a family. We had to have you in the picture."

God, his mouth was desert dry. "You've changed your mind."

Her finger stopped moving, but she didn't switch her gaze to his face. "Even with a player in all the right positions, you can't call yourself a family. I finally realize that."

He grunted. That was all he could get out around the pain tightening in his chest.

"Only love can do that," she said, her voice almost a whisper. "Only the desire to be together."

The rain pounded on the roof as if it wanted to come in, but only silence entered.

After long moments, Katie cleared her throat. "I overheard you talking to Dan about Iceland."

Seth's pulse jumped. "Katie—"

She put up a hand. "I think you should make your

trip now. No need to wait for the babies to be born." That hand crept over her belly. "We're going to be just fine by ourselves."

"Katie—"

"Can you honestly say that you want to stay?" Her blue eyes lasered into his.

That's a trick question! he wanted to shout. But the pain on her face stopped him. "This is exactly what I didn't want." The words felt torn from his throat. "I never wanted to hurt you."

The corners of her mouth lifted in a half smile. "I know. You're still one of the good guys."

Seth pinched the bridge of his nose. "I told you I'd stay, Katie. I don't break promises. I'll be with you as long as you need me. As long as you want me."

She half laughed. "I know all that, too. But I want more, Seth. More than obligations and a willingness to take on a responsibility. You should want more, too."

He shook his head. "I never wanted a wife and children. I never saw that for myself."

"Maybe that's why it will never work."

The pain in Seth's chest twisted, taking away his air. He forced a long breath into his lungs. "What do you want, Katie? What do you want me to do?"

"I want you to follow your heart, Seth. And if it says go to Iceland, then go, and go now. I think it will hurt less, for both of us, that way."

The rain echoed in his head, pounding, pounding. "My father left, too, Katie. And it hurt like hell."

Her gaze remained on his face.

He took in another slow breath. "I wouldn't want to do that to the twins. Be there...and then be gone." Hadn't he always worried that it would come to this? Maybe it *would* be better if he left now.

But he couldn't say the words.

It didn't matter; she read them on his face. The sad acceptance in her voice twisted his gut. "I'll stay with Izzy and Dan for a few days. They won't mind, and it will give you some time to clear out of the house and get on that plane."

He ran a hand through his hair. "I *never* wanted to hurt you, Katie."

She smiled that half-sad, half-serene smile again. "You've taught me a lot, Seth. I'm seeing my childhood clearly for the first time. And I have a new definition of family."

Numb, he left the house quickly. It wasn't until he'd backed the car out of the driveway that he realized she hadn't denied he'd caused her pain.

I'm doing the right thing, Seth thought. God, that refrain was becoming nauseatingly familiar. It had been the right thing to let Katie marry someone else and let him adopt the babies. The right thing for Seth to marry her himself. The right thing for him to leave.

Whoosh-squeak, whoosh-squeak. The Explorer's windshield wipers offered no wisdom as they valiantly tried sweeping away the sheets of rain. Seth braked the car gently around another corner of the mountain road. To block out his thoughts, he turned on the radio and idly switched between the ''Dr. Dog'' question-and-answer show and the broadcast of the UC Berkeley football game.

''Go, Bears,'' he said with a nod to Ryan's alma mater.

Ryan. What would his brother think of this latest development?

''I tried, Ry, really I did.''

Whoosh-squeak, whoosh-squeak.

''You left me holding the bag again, you know.'' A spurt of irritation at his brother heated his mood. Seth braked around another curve.

''Remember our neighbor, old Mrs. Richie? The lady with the killer slope of a lawn? Yeah, you'd tell her, 'Seth and I will mow for you.' You'd do the flat part up by the house, and my half would be the hill leading to the road. With the rocks that'd kick up in your face about every two minutes.''

Whoosh-squeak.

Seth gripped the steering wheel and felt the irritation leap to anger. ''Oh, yeah, and when those hookers were hanging around the corner near the Ends of the Earth offices. You told the Community Association we'd take care of it. But was it you that ran them out of there?''

Seth snorted. ''No way. Uh-uh. You left it up to little brother to talk those ladies into moving out of the neighborhood.''

Seth's blood began to a boil. ''Yeah, Ry, you left it up to me, damn it.'' Almost out of breath with frustration, Seth spoke over the sportscaster, the windshield wipers and his own raging conscience. "It's either the hills, the whores, or the babies, Ryan, and this time I'm saying no."

A bell rang, as if his anger had reached jackpot level. It took another ring for him to realize the sound came from the car's cell phone.

He picked it up. "Yeah. Cooper."

"Seth."

It was Katie's voice, and something in that one word told him she wasn't calling to get him back.

He ignored the wave of disappointment. "What's the matter?"

She hesitated. He could almost see her biting her bottom lip.

He gripped the wheel and steered around another curve. "What is it, Katie?"

"Are you having any trouble on the road?" she asked. "Any signs of traffic?"

"Traffic?" Sure, there was only this one road in and out of the area, but he'd only occasionally glimpsed the taillights of another car in the entire twenty minutes since he'd left.

"We've heard there may be a mud slide up ahead."

Seth groaned. "Damn. I haven't seen anything yet, but I'll keep my eyes open. Thanks for the warning." As if he'd been duly cautioned, the rain started beating against the hood of the car even harder. "The weather's hell out here, that's for sure."

He could hear the muffled tones of Katie relating the news. "Seth—"

He interrupted her. "I'll be fine, Katie. Don't you worry. Tell Izzy and Dan not to worry, either."

An ironic note entered Katie's voice. "That may be a little problem."

Seth eased up on the accelerator. "Tell Izzy I'm slowing down as we speak. Dan knows I'm a good driver."

"Oh, it's not you they're worried about." Katie's voice had gone from anxious, to ironic, to strangely calm. "We think Izzy's having the baby."

"*What?*"

"The baby. And Dan is threatening to faint or throw up or both. The doctor told us there's a major mud slide between here and the hospital." She paused, then went on. "Oh, yeah, and the medivac helicopters can't fly in this kind of weather."

Seth felt cold sweat pop out on his upper lip. "Anything else?" Now the irony was in his voice.

That eerie calmness was still in hers. "Let me see. The baby, Dan, the possible mud slide, and no helicopter. Nope, I think that about covers it."

Seth peered ahead. Red taillights. More red taillights. Not a one was moving. "Sorry, Beauty, there *is* just a bit more. I'm here to confirm your possible mud slide. And traffic. I see lots and lots of both."

10

➤━◆━◀

With taillights ahead of him and a crisis behind him, Seth braked and turned the wheel. "Hang on, Katie," he said, and clicked off the phone. Then he completed the U-turn and headed away from the line of traffic and the mud slide. Back to Katie.

Back to an imminent birth.

He gripped the steering wheel with both hands and accelerated as fast as the continued rain and wet road would let him. *What the hell am I doing?*

I'll watch the pot boil, he told himself.

Stack clean towels.

But he couldn't just drive off and leave Katie—and his friends—facing an emergency.

Wind-driven rain whipped his face after leaving his car in Izzy and Dan's driveway. The afternoon was as dark as dusk as he pounded on the door, then pushed it open.

Nobody met him in the entryway. His gut tightened, and he looked in the direction of the master bedroom. At the end of the long hallway, light showed beneath the door.

He didn't belong in there. He didn't want to go in there.

"Katie? Dan?" he called from where he was.

At the bedroom door, a wedge of light widened. Katie came toward him, her face flushed. She smiled faintly. "For a minute I thought the paramedics might have made it."

The wedge widened more as Dan came flying down the hallway, then slid to a stop. "Oh, God," he said, the whites of his eyes showing. "Oh, God." He gulped visibly. "You're not a doctor, are you Seth?"

Dumbfounded, Seth stared at his buddy.

Katie half smiled. "Welcome to Panic General."

Dan came forward to make a death grip on Seth's forearm. "You gotta get me out of here. I gotta go somewhere."

Seth pried Dan's fingers off his arm. "Not right now, Dan." He slanted a look at Katie. "How's Izzy?"

"Much calmer than Daddy, here. But we just lost contact with the doctor. The phones are out."

Seth's stomach tightened again. "I'll get the cell phone from the Explorer."

"Let me do it," Dan's voice rasped. "I'll get the phone." He was out the front door in seconds.

Katie looked down the hall toward the master bedroom. "I've got to get back to Izzy. Do you want to come in and see her? The distraction might help a little."

"No." The word was out before he even thought it. "But I boil a mean pot of water," he offered.

Her smile didn't budge the worry lines between her eyes. "That's just the movies." She started down the hall, then paused. "Really, you can come in. We're trying to talk about other things between contractions."

Contractions. Seth tightened his hands into fists. "No, no. I wouldn't be any good in there." He tried relaxing his hands, and failed. "But call me if you need something else."

Katie disappeared down the hall.

Unsure what else to do, Seth sat on the living-room sofa, listening to the wind howl about the house. Anxiety pushed him back to his feet. Hell. Maybe he shouldn't have returned. Boiling water wasn't required and he certainly wasn't going to provide any other kind of help.

Hurried footsteps sounded from the hallway. Katie rushed into the living room. "Where's Dan? Izzy wants to make sure we can get through on the cell phone."

Where *was* Dan? "I'll get him." Without even bothering with his coat, Seth forced the front door open, pushing it against a heavy blast of rain and wind. He found Dan in the driver's seat of the Explorer, his eyes closed.

Seth climbed into the passenger seat. "What are you doing, Dan? They need the cell phone."

Without opening his eyes, Dan handed the phone

over. "Gimme your keys, Seth. I need to go out for a beer."

"What?" Seth's voice croaked like a frog's. "Your wife is having a baby in there."

"I can't help her. I gotta get out of here. Gimme your keys."

"I'll give you a black eye if you don't get out of the car, you jerk." Seth tried laughing, hoping Dan was joking around, too.

He opened his eyes and shook his head slowly. "I can't help her, man."

Anger rose in Seth, moving upward from his toes. "You're not abandoning Izzy now, Dan," he said threateningly. "Not if I have to hog-tie you and carry you in there myself."

Wet wind rushed into the car as Dan opened the door. "I'm going for a walk."

Seth grabbed his friend's arm and leaned over to pull the door shut. "No, you're not." He kept his hand around Dan's forearm. "Izzy needs you. You have to stick it out for Izzy."

Beneath Seth's hand, Dan's arm was hard as a rock. "There's supposed to be a doctor, Seth. Nurses. Metal beds. All the right stuff."

Seth opened the passenger door and tightened his grip on Dan's arm. "The only 'right stuff' Izzy needs now is you," he said. He hauled Dan across the seats, pulling the other man in the direction of the house. "It's time to take care of Izzy."

Without loosening his grip, Seth got Dan into the

house. When Dan looked longingly back at the front door, Seth rolled his eyes and led him to the master bedroom. "Get in there," he commanded his friend.

Dan turned to stone. With an inward groan, Seth lightly knocked on the bedroom door, then opened it and pushed Dan through. "Make room for Daddy," he called out softly.

Dan took a step inside, then turned into granite again. With a muttered curse, Seth stepped through the doorway, too, and with his hands on Dan's shoulders, propelled him toward the bed.

Izzy sat up against a mound of pillows, her face white except for her flurry of rusty freckles. "Excuse me," Seth said, feeling a flush crawl up his neck. "But Dan just needed a little help."

Katie walked in from the attached bath, a wet washcloth in her hand. She gave Seth a grateful look, then pointed Dan toward a chair beside the bed. "Dan, sit there beside Izzy." She spoke slowly and calmly, in a voice that didn't brook argument. "Hold her hand. Be comforting. *Be there.*"

Amazingly, Dan did as instructed.

Seth started backing out of the room. Then Katie rounded on him. "Wait."

His heart stilled. Surely—

"The cell phone," she said.

He breathed again, and reached into his pocket and handed over the phone. Their fingers brushed in the exchange.

Even now, her touch ran through his body. He could almost taste the sensation on his tongue.

"You're staying, too," she said.

He heard it through the haze of awareness. "Wha—" He swallowed. "What?"

She reached out to grip his hand. "I need you, Seth," she whispered. "I...I'm afraid. I don't want to do this by myself and Dan isn't going to be any help."

A cold wave rolled down Seth's spine. But Katie's hand was cold, too, and he suddenly, more than anything, needed to warm her. "Okay," he found himself saying. "I'm here." He squeezed her hand strongly. "I'm right here."

Childbirth was spectacular. Messy. A miracle. Katie placed the blanket-wrapped baby boy on Izzy's chest and stared at mother and child with satisfaction. "You did it, Iz," she said. "Great job."

Izzy smiled down at the baby, then looked up at Dan, who stroked a finger wonderingly down the infant's cheek. "That wasn't so bad, was it, darling?"

Katie felt the weight of Seth's palm against her hair. "*You* did a great job, Katie," he said in her ear.

What a crock. Katie's breath left her lungs and a fresh tear coursed down her cheek. In fact, it had been Seth who had performed the actual delivery as Katie listened to and repeated the instructions received over the cell phone.

"My hands are bigger," he'd said, and he'd eased

the baby into the world, suctioning out the mouth and nose, tying off the umbilical cord—all with fingers so steady that they belied the tension she saw in the line of his jaw and the set of his shoulders.

Dan looked up at Katie, his eyes bright and his entire face flushed. "Isn't he beautiful? Isn't he the smartest, funniest, most handsome boy in all the world?"

Katie and Izzy laughed together. "Just like his dad," Katie agreed.

Dan smiled even more broadly. His gaze turned to Seth. "I'm a father. I have a son."

Seth smiled back, his grin so warm that Katie felt its heat against her skin.

"Way to go, buddy. Way to go," Seth said.

The cell phone buzzed and Seth picked it up and listened briefly. His smile widened further as he clicked off. "Good news, everybody. They cleared away part of the mud slide. Paramedics and an ambulance are on the way."

Dan whooped. "I know everything's fine, but I'll feel better when the doctor has seen Izzy and—" He looked down at his wife. "I forget the name we picked out."

Seth grinned again. "Seth would do just fine."

Katie shoved at his shoulder playfully. "Wait a minute. I'm sure there's a male form of Katherine...."

Seth groaned. "Watch out, guys, she'll be wanting to name your kid Kumquat or something." He slung his arm around her shoulder. "Hey, my middle name is Alexander. You could use that, and…"

Katie tuned out the rest of the joking conversation and focused on the feel of Seth's arm around her.

The warm, strong weight both held her up and tore her apart. She inhaled a long breath, savoring his touch for one last time. With only a fingernail-hold on her emotional control, it was time she moved away from him.

Having Seth come back after their goodbye hadn't been painful. She'd been relieved to have someone she could count on in the crisis. But now that Izzy and Dan's son had been born, it was time to back away from him again.

It was time for another—their last—goodbye.

She took in a second long breath as the other three kept laughing about baby names. Soon, her babies would be in her arms. Thanks to Seth, she'd learned she didn't need a man—a father—to complete their circle.

What would make her and the twins happy was her love for them, and her determination to be a good mother. Her dedication to them would define the three of them as a family.

Seth squeezed her shoulders again and smiled down at her. "Right?"

She pasted on a smile and nodded back without knowing what she was agreeing to. He would be leaving soon, and the best she could hope for was to continue smiling as he drove away.

He glanced down at her again, and as if the pain in her heart was written all over her face, his smile died. He leaned toward her, and she read the kiss on *his* face.

No.

She backed away and slipped out of his reach. If he kissed her, she would make a big mistake. Like ask him to stay.

Like tell him she loved him.

She couldn't let that happen.

The ambulance and paramedics arrived and after a brief spate of activity, Dan, Izzy and the baby were loaded into the ambulance. Both Seth and Katie had promised to visit them in the hospital. Dan, drunk with exhilaration, was promising the baby would be named Sate or Keth.

Katie hoped a cooler head—Izzy's—would prevail.

And then the front door shut and the silence was only broken by the *plink, plink, plink* of the rain on the roof and the sound of Katie's heartbeat in her ears.

"Well." Seth shoved his hands through his hair and then shoved his hands in his pockets.

"Well." Katie wished she had pockets. But her leggings and maternity top didn't leave any place to put her hands. She knotted them together in front of her, then put them behind her back.

"Well." His hands raked through his hair again. He shuffled from foot to foot, looking endearingly awkward.

Katie took a firm grip of her heart. It would be so

easy to tell him she loved him. So easy to let her heart go to mush over the man.

"I guess—"

"You should be going," Katie finished for him. It would be best for them both. Leave quickly. Do it. *Go,* she urged him silently. *While I still can keep this secret to myself.*

"I want to talk first." Seth moved from the entryway toward the living room.

Katie lingered by the front door. "It's late," she said. "Why don't you go ahead and—"

He patted the spot on the sofa beside him. "Katie. Please come talk to me."

Her feet moved without her permission. She only hoped her tongue wouldn't, as well.

She chose to sit in the chair opposite him instead of on the sofa beside him. She sat primly, hoping he would sense her reluctance and leave.

"Katie, I don't want to go."

So much for sensing her reluctance. She sighed. "Seth..." If only she could believe he wanted to stay for some reason other than obligation.

"Today... The birth..." He gestured vaguely. "You'll be alone if I go."

She popped up from her chair and wished she could get him to move as easily. "I'll be fine, Seth."

He groaned. "Somehow I knew you'd say that."

"What else *can* I say?" she asked, her frustration clear in her voice. "How can I make you understand that what we have isn't what I want?"

Now he stood and strode over to her. "I know you, Katie." He cupped her cheek with his wide, hard palm. "Even if you needed me, I don't think you'd ask me to stay."

Beneath his hand, Katie's skin prickled and goose bumps ran down her neck. The sound of her heart was like a roar in her ears. She knew what she could tell him. She knew if she bared her heart he would walk away from her. "You've got it all wrong," she whispered. "Backward, actually."

Maybe he could feel the reaction of her skin. Maybe, finally, he could sense what she had to say. His hand dropped, and he took a step back. "What do I have wrong?"

"I don't *need* you," she said, her voice hoarse. "To be honest, I *love* you." The roaring turned into a dizzying whine. "And because I want someone who will love me in return, I'm letting you go."

His face turned hard. More set than it had been during those tension-filled moments when he'd eased a brand-new baby into the world. "You love me?" He said the words as if he couldn't take in their meaning.

Nothing world-shattering happened after that. She hadn't expected it to. She'd expected what *did* happen.

Seth walked out of the living room. Seth put on his coat. Seth drove out of her life.

Seth loaded up the car with his gifts for Izzy and Dan's baby. He put them right beside his trusty duffel and backpack, pulled from the closet at Katie's, then packed with all the essentials for his old life.

His life pre-Katie.

He jumped into the driver's seat and started the car, then backed out of Katie's driveway, not pausing for one last look. Not giving the home one last thought.

Because he hadn't for one minute stopped thinking of her anyway. Not since she'd told him those three small words.

He knew why she'd said she loved him. If she told him that and *still* asked him to go, then she must really mean it. She honestly wanted him out of her life.

Isn't that what he wanted, too?

He didn't want to leave the babies, though. In time, when some of the rawness had passed, he would talk to her about that. Through telegram or fax or telephone, they would talk about his relationship to the twins.

The hospital where he would find Izzy and her new son wasn't far away, and not much farther from that was the hotel where he planned to live until he could schedule the Iceland trip. He squinted as the morning sun split a gray cloud to dazzle his tired eyes.

He'd heard every chime of the grandfather clock in the hallway the night before. In Katie's bed with Katie's pillow underneath his head, her perfume, not sleep, had overtaken him. Yeah, he could have gone back to the sterility of the guest bedroom...but he hadn't.

Seth pulled into the hospital visitors' lot and parked. Katie was smart to insist he leave. Out of the car, he unlocked the back door of the Explorer. If she loved him, he had the power to mess up her life. He might disappoint her. Abandon her, lea—

He stared at the luggage in the back of the car. Leave her. Like he was doing already.

Gritting his teeth, Seth grasped the gifts and slammed shut the car door, then used his difficulty in locating the maternity wing as an excuse not to think of anything else.

But then he stood in front of room 4459, yellow roses in one hand, a rattle-filled football in the other, and heard a baby's cry, Izzy's murmur, Dan's soft chuckle.

Katie's grandfather clock started tolling in his head again like a warning, an alarm that he needed to pay attention to.

Wake up. Take heed.

The wide hospital-room door swung open and Dan stepped out. "Hey, buddy, what's up—?"

"My father walked away from it all," Seth said, his pulse pounding at his temples in rhythm with the clock chimes he continued to hear in his head.

To his credit, Dan didn't put into words the questions written all over his face. "Yeah."

"He never came back. Never called. I have no way of telling him about...Ryan. About the twins."

"Yeah," Dan said again.

"*I'd* want to know," Seth said emphatically. "I always want to know what—how—they're doing. The twins."

A frown appeared between Dan's brows. "You will, buddy."

Seth shook his head. "And Katie. I always want to know how Katie's doing." He put his hand on Dan's forearm. "You'll tell me, won't you Dan? If I call you, you'll tell me how she is?"

"If I can—" A fretful whimper came from the hospital room and Dan glanced back. "But you'll be right there, buddy. A little father-to-be panic doesn't mean—"

Another cry from the baby caused Dan to turn around. "I'll be right back," he said, and disappeared into the room.

Seth didn't move. *A little father-to-be panic.* Dan didn't have a clue. He wasn't panicking about fatherhood. If he was panicking at all, it was about love.

The pounding in his head suddenly stopped.

If he was panicking at all, it was about... His grip tightened so hard on the flowers that a thorn pricked him through the tissue and plastic coverings.

It was about being in love with Katie.

Katie inhaled a deep sigh and unlocked the door to her candy kitchen. After a day of emotional upheavals and a night without sleep, she'd wanted to get back home as soon as possible. With Dan's permission, she'd borrowed one of their cars and headed home this morning, promising herself that if Seth's car was in the driveway she would hang out at the local coffee bar until she could be sure he was at the office.

There'd been no Explorer in the drive, but the steam on the bathroom mirror and the scent of his after-shave in the bedroom told her she'd just missed him. She'd learned something else, as well—Seth was gone, permanently, from the house. His clothes were missing from the drawers and closet, and his luggage was gone, as well.

She had her place to herself again.

Her gaze roamed the empty candy kitchen and the windows that looked out toward the even-emptier house.

She'd never been so lonely in her life.

But she had candy orders to complete, and a special order for a friend's daughter's birthday. Tying on an apron, Katie decided to make popcorn-balls-on-a-stick and heavenly hash using colored marshmallows, peanuts and milk chocolate. Both should appeal to children.

With the air popper clattering as it spit popcorn into a huge plastic bowl, Katie nearly missed the knocking on the kitchen door. She took a step toward the sound, then stopped. Without even opening the door, she sensed who stood behind it.

"Damn," she said, then looked guiltily down at her abdomen. "Sorry, guys."

Another spurt of banging on the door. With slow

feet, Katie moved toward it. She didn't want to see him again. Not for a while, anyway.

"Yes?" she called through the door. "Who's there?"

"It's me."

His rough voice sent a shiver down her back. The shiver made her mad. *You've to get over him,* she told herself. "Me, who?"

"Me, Seth, dammit."

Seth Dammit sounded frustrated. Good.

"What do you want?" Maybe he'd misplaced his passport. Or maybe he was looking for those holey socks she'd thrown out. With luck it would be something she could handle through the door.

"I want to talk to you."

She could tell he was trying to be patient. She liked the effort it was costing him.

"I'm listening."

"For God's sake, Katie, let me in. This is stupid."

It *was* pretty stupid, but it also felt pretty good. Yelling at him through the doorway beat looking at him, wanting him, yearning for everything she could never have. But she unlocked the door and swung it open anyway.

At that moment, the air popper ceased its rattle, so Katie didn't even meet Seth's eyes before turning back to the counter, refilling the popper's reservoir and switching the appliance back on. With the homey smell of hot popcorn in her nose, and the distracting *pop-pop-pop* in her ears, she swung back toward him.

"Passport, top drawer of the bureau in the guest bedroom," she said. "Holey socks, out with the garbage two weeks ago."

"What?" He didn't look any better than she did. His hair was finger-rumpled and his green eyes troubled-looking.

She still wanted to hold him against her breast and demand he be hers forever.

She put on a grim smile. "I'm just guessing at why you're here."

A vee settled between his eyebrows.

"What you left behind," she said helpfully.

He laughed shortly and his hand clapped over his heart. "I *know* what I left behind. I've not come back for that. I've come back to tell you..." He shuffled his feet and looked over her shoulder at the noisy air popper. "Can you turn that thing off?"

What Katie wanted to turn off was the equally-staccato beating of her heart. He came back to tell her—what? What could he say that could make this any easier?

Nothing.

"It will be done in a minute," she said, afraid that in silence he would hear her slamming heartbeat. "Just talk over it."

With a sigh, he crossed his arms over his chest. "I'm not leaving," he said.

She grimaced. "All right, all right. I'll turn it off, if that's what it takes." But as she turned, he grabbed her wrist. Traitorously hot streaks of sensation shot toward her shoulder.

"No," he said. "I mean I'm not leaving town. No Iceland."

Katie looked into his eyes—really looked into them for the first time since he'd come into the kitchen. She'd thought they were troubled, but now they appeared wary...and determined. "We've had this conversation already, Seth."

"*You* had your say. I...didn't say much of anything."

Well, that was true. But she didn't want to hear it now. "I know what you want to tell me." She stepped away from his touch and stared down at her toes, which she certainly wouldn't have sight of for much longer.

"You think you should stay. Help me through the rest of the pregnancy. Be there at the childbirth, which, I fervently pray, will be in a delivery room. You think you should do your share of diaper changing and 3:00 a.m. feedings."

"That's right, but—"

"But I don't want a hero, Seth. I want a husband." Her voice sounded scratchy, and she swallowed to smooth it out.

"I want to be your husband."

She wiped her palms against her apron. "I know what we experienced yesterday was intense...and scary. But I can do it by myself, Seth. I know I'm strong enough."

He smiled. "I know you can, too. I do, Katie," he said over her protest. "When we first married, I admit I saw you like I'd seen my mother. I thought you needed a man. But I know you could do it alone. I wouldn't have even gotten this far away for a minute if I didn't believe that."

His confidence in her sent a wash of warmth running through her. "The twins—"

"Would be fine if they had only you, Katie. You could do a great job with them. But I want to be in their lives—"

"And you can. We'll work out something—" Katie turned just as the popcorn began overflowing the bowl. She rushed to the counter and slid an empty bowl beneath the popper.

"And I want to be in your life, too, Katie." She heard his words over the final staccato bursts of the popper. "I love you."

"What?" She gripped the countertop, staring at her white knuckles.

Then he was behind her, his warm, strong chest at her back, his big hands covering hers. "I'm in love with you."

She didn't turn around. She didn't want to look at him and see the good intentions—and the lie—in his eyes. "You don't," she whispered. "Please don't say you do."

He pulled her back against him, cradling her in the warmth of his arms. "But I do, Beauty. It just took me too long to realize it."

She felt his chin rest on top of her head. Her heart beat painfully hard in her chest as if it believed him. Silly thing. "You never saw a wife and children in your future," she reminded them both.

He turned her in his arms, and when she still wouldn't look at him, he lifted her chin with his hand. "Because I was afraid, Katie. All that big talk about thinking I would be like my father and hurt you some-day was all a cowardly cover."

The green in his eyes was the green of everything living—like spring grass, and dappled forests, and dark, cool oceans where mysteries and promises dwelled. "A cover for what?" she whispered.

"For my own fears. If I loved—if I loved *you*—then I could be hurt, too. You could leave me behind like my father did. Like my mother left Ryan and me behind emotionally. Like Ryan left me just a few months ago."

Katie found herself stroking his cheek. Against her palm his skin was warm, familiar, maybe even hers. "I won't leave you," she said.

The green in his eyes blazed, like the flash of sunset on the ocean. "I'm willing to risk it," he said.

"Me—" She meant to add "too," but his mouth came down before she could finish. She melted in his arms, kissing the man of her soul, embracing the promise of the life she'd always wanted; and the smell of chocolate and nuts and popcorn would always be inextricably entwined with the wonder of love.

And for the rest of her life, her candies always tasted the better for it.

EPILOGUE

—■—◆—

Flowers crowded the phone on the bedside table. A stuffed-animal zoo had taken up residence at the bottom of Katie's hospital bed. A lone balloon, escapee from the bouquet tied to one of the room's chairs, hovered like a guardian angel between the two clear isolettes.

Katie, happy but exhausted, smiled at her absolutely chipper-looking husband. "I can't stand how perky you are." She pasted on a pretend frown. "You could at least have the decency to get some dark circles under your eyes."

Seth looked up from his contemplation of the two tiny beings snoozing in their wrapping of soft flannel blankets. "Did you say something to me, Beauty?"

She shook her head fondly. "I'm not sure I like this competition." To belie her words, she sighed and said, "They *are* the most perfect darlings ever, right?"

Seth trailed his hand down her cheek, then leaned over to softly kiss her mouth. "As perfect and as darling as their mommy."

Katie captured his hand and held it against her face. "I felt them with us, Seth." She searched his eyes. "Ryan and Karen were here last night."

He squeezed her fingers. "I know," he said quietly. "I felt happiness...and peace."

Katie blinked away the tears. This was a moment for smiles. "And I'll feel a whole lot better when we get this paperwork filled out." She patted the stack of sheets on her lap. "Do it for me, honey, will you?"

Seth obligingly lifted the papers and pen from the hospital blanket. "If I have to give them my Social Security number one more time—" He stopped, a frown wrinkling his brow. "This is the paperwork for the birth certificates."

"Yep." Katie nodded, avoiding Seth's eyes by watching the fascinating facial movements of her firstborn. Then she had to give equal attention to her second-born. "You fill out the names for me."

Seth had remained obstinately distant when it came to deciding on the twins' names. Whatever she wanted, he'd always said, although he'd been quick to nix anything particularly outrageous.

"I don't know, Katie...."

She glanced over and saw him with the pen poised above the paper.

He cleared his throat. "If I name them, they'll— they'll belong to me."

She smiled back serenely. "But they already do, Seth. We all do."

Seth stared at the woman who had brought everything to his life—happiness, home, children.

Children.

In his heart, he made a solemn promise to each of them. *I'll always be here for you,* he thought, looking at each small face in turn.

Then he swung toward his wife, her beauty never so heart-wrenching than this moment. "God, I love you," he said, as if it was a prayer.

And she smiled that smile again, and watched him name their babies on the little white form that proclaimed them his before all the world. Because, as she'd said, his wife and the babies *were* his.

Katie...and Angela and Rose.

*   *   *   *   *

Return to the Towers!

In March
New York Times bestselling author

NORA ROBERTS

brings us to the Calhouns' fabulous
Maine coast mansion and reveals the
tragic secrets hidden there for generations.

For all his degrees, Professor Max Quartermain has a
lot to learn about love—and luscious Lilah Calhoun is
just the woman to teach him. Ex-cop Holt Bradford is
as prickly as a thornbush—until Suzanna Calhoun's
special touch makes love blossom in his heart.
And all of them are caught in the race to solve
the generations-old mystery of a priceless
lost necklace…and a timeless love.

Lilah and Suzanna
THE
Calhoun Women

**A special 2-in-1 edition containing
FOR THE LOVE OF LILAH and
SUZANNA'S SURRENDER**

Available at your favorite retail outlet.

Take 4 bestselling love stories FREE

Plus get a FREE surprise gift!

Special Limited-time Offer

Mail to Silhouette Reader Service™

3010 Walden Avenue
P.O. Box 1867
Buffalo, N.Y. 14269-1867

YES! Please send me 4 free Silhouette Yours Truly™ novels and my free surprise gift. Then send me 4 brand-new novels every other month, which I will receive months before they appear in bookstores. Bill me at the low price of $2.69 each plus 25¢ delivery and applicable sales tax, if any.* That's the complete price and a savings of over 10% off the cover prices—quite a bargain! I understand that accepting the books and gift places me under no obligation ever to buy any books. I can always return a shipment and cancel at any time. Even if I never buy another book from Silhouette, the 4 free books and the surprise gift are mine to keep forever.

201 BPA AZH2

Name	(PLEASE PRINT)
Address	Apt. No.
City	State	Zip

This offer is limited to one order per household and not valid to present Silhouette Yours Truly™ subscribers. *Terms and prices are subject to change without notice. Sales tax applicable in N.Y.

RETURN TO WHITEHORN

Silhouette's beloved **MONTANA MAVERICKS** returns with brand-new stories from your favorite authors! Welcome back to Whitehorn, Montana—a place where rich tales of passion and adventure are unfolding under the Big Sky. The new generation of Mavericks will leave you breathless!

Coming from Silhouette Special Edition°:

February 98: LETTER TO A LONESOME COWBOY by Jackie Merritt

March 98: WIFE MOST WANTED by Joan Elliott Pickart

May 98: A FATHER'S VOW by Myrna Temte

June 98: A HERO'S HOMECOMING by Laurie Paige

And don't miss these two very special additions to the Montana Mavericks saga:

MONTANA MAVERICKS WEDDINGS
by Diana Palmer, Ann Major and Susan Mallery
Short story collection available April 98

WILD WEST WIFE by Susan Mallery
Harlequin Historicals available July 98

Round up these great new stories
at your favorite retail outlet.

Silhouette®   Look us up on-line at: http://www.romance.net

SSEMMF-J

SANDRA STEFFEN

Continues the
twelve-book series—
36 Hours—in February 1998
with Book Eight

MARRIAGE BY CONTRACT

Nurse Bethany Kent could think of only one man who could
make her dream come true: Dr. Tony Petrocelli, the man who
had helped her save the life of the infant she desperately
wanted to adopt. As husband and wife, they could provide the
abandoned baby with a loving home. But could they provide
each other with more than just a convenient marriage?

For Tony and Bethany and *all* the residents of Grand Springs,
Colorado, the storm-induced blackout was just the beginning
of 36 Hours that changed *everything!* You won't want to miss a
single book.

Available at your favorite retail outlet.

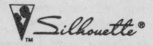